Russkaya Mafiya Spin-Off

By: International Bestselling Author Sapphire Knight

Melissa thank you!

Sapphie Knight

Sapphire Knight

Undercover Intentions

Copyright © 2017 by Sapphire Knight

Cover Design by CT Cover Creations

Editing by Mitzi Carroll

Formatting by Brenda Wright – Formatting Done Wright

Undercover Intentions

Table of Contents

ACKNOWLEDGEMENTS

My husband - I love you more than words can express. Thank you for the support you've shown me.

My boys - You are my whole world. I love you both. This never changes, and you better not be reading these books until you're thirty and tell yourself your momma did not write them!

My Beta Babes - Wendi Stacilaucki-Hunsicker and Patti Novia West. Thank you for all the love you've shown me. You've all helped me grow tremendously in my writing, and I'm forever grateful. This wouldn't be possible without your input and suggestions.

Editor Mitzi Carroll – Your hard work makes mine stand out, and I'm so grateful! Thank you for pouring tons of hours into my passion and being so wonderful to me. One day I'll meet you and one day I'll squishy hug you!

Cover Designer CT Cover Creations - Thank you sooo much! Your creativity is amazing and always leaves me speechless! Thank you tons for your continued support and friendship.

Photographer Eric Battershell - Thank you so much for the amazing support and friendship you have been kind enough to give me. I look forward to our future collaborations.

Model Kaz van der Waard – Thank you for being on my cover. You capture my characters as a whole, beautifully.

Formatter Brenda Wright – Thank you for making my work look professional and beautiful. I truly appreciate it and the kindness you've shown me.

My Blogger Friends –YOU ARE AMAZING! I LOVE YOU! No really, I do!!! You take a new chance on me with each book and in return share my passion with the world. You never truly get enough credit, and I'm forever grateful!

My Readers – I love you. You make my life possible, thank you.

COMMON TERMS

Moy – My

Sin – Son

Brat – Brother

Nyet – No

Da – Yes

Saystraa – Sister

Spaseeba – Thank you

Russkaya Mafiya – Russian Mafiya

THIS IS NOT A MAFIA BOOK.

This is a spin-off of from my Russkaya Mafiya series, but it is a standalone. There is mafia-ish stuff going on, but I repeat-this is not a full-blown mafia book! Thank you for reading, I hope you enjoy.

DEDICATION

To Meili, Loki, Ares, and Bella.

It's amazing I got this book finished with how much you assholes barked through it. Regardless, I love my Dobermans. Do a good deed, donate to an animal rescue and make a difference in the world.

WARNING

This novel includes graphic language and adult situations. It may be offensive to some readers and includes situations that may be hotspots for certain individuals. This book is intended for ages 18 and older due to some steamy spots. This work is fictional. The story is meant to entertain the reader and may not always be completely accurate. Any reproduction of these works without Author Sapphire Knight's written consent is pirating and will be punished to the fullest extent of the law.

Sapphire Knight

This is a standalone but can be read with the Russkaya Mafiya series also:

Secrets

Corrupted

Unwanted Sacrifices

Russian Roulette box set

Undercover Intentions

PROLOGUE

Sasha

I hate this man standing beside The Master. I hate him so much; I wish he would choke on his own spit and die. The things Yema does to us—to me—are sickening. I thought the man from last weekend was going to take me away, but Yema wouldn't allow it. I swear he only did it so he could get another week to degrade me further.

"Girl!" It's said with distaste by The Master. As if I'm the scum on the bottom of their shoes.

I never understood why they put us through all of this if they hate us so much. Why keep us prisoner? Why keep us locked up, away from other people? You'd think if we were such a burden, they'd kick us to the street. I often wish they would. I'd much rather sleep on a dirty street curb than here—on clean sheets—only to be roused whenever one of them is bored or angry.

"He said, 'Girl'!" the mean one yells again. This time a bookend flies toward my head. It crashes against the wall beside me, and I swear fury fills Yema's eyes at the loud thump it makes hitting the drywall.

"Yes, Master? How can I serve you?" I go to him, dropping to my knees in front of him — pretending to worship him — as he wishes us to do. He thinks he's the creator of all things, the one to offer us life, The Master.

He's wrong. I remember my mother, the one who filled my heart with warmth and safety. I never had to fear her when she raised her hand or called my name.

My name...I can't even remember my real name anymore. Was it Sasha? Or did they just pick a new Russian name and make me believe it belonged to me all along?

"I don't see why anyone would want you with how slow you are." He scowls, his cold, beady eyes glaring down at me.

Even full of bitterness, his features are handsome. Maybe because I don't ever remember having a father, and this man has given me what little I do have? The others here I hate, like Yema...They touch and hurt me whenever they feel like it. It's been so long now; I don't even get sick from it anymore. I just make it fade away.

I remain quiet as I'm supposed to. I'm not allowed to speak. Sometimes I'll mess up, but I try not to. His hand comes hard and fast when I don't mind his rules.

Is it the businessman from the event who's interested in me? Could he be talking about the tattooed man who looked at Yema like he wanted to cut his throat from one side to the other? The handsome one?

I hope so. He wasn't friendly, but he had kind eyes. I've met very few men with a kindness shining in them as he had.

"You need to be ready for tonight. Go to the basement and prepare yourself. Do not make Yema wait for you."

"Yes, Master," I reply, staring at his feet until he's turned away and my gaze is met with the fur from the rug I'm kneeling on. Only once he's turned his back to me, do I stand and make my way to the basement.

Yema promised Mr. Masterson that he could take me this weekend. I've prayed every morning and every night that he remembers, that he comes back for me. He took Trixie, the angel-haired one last weekend. But that's okay. I'll be his new favorite, I know it and if not...I'll kill her.

Sapphire Knight

The officer said, "You drinking?"

I said, "You buying?"

We just laughed and laughed.

I need bail money.

-Funny Meme

"Yeah?"

"Have you found Natasha yet?"

"Nyet." Sighing, I replace the rocks glass of vodka back on the shiny, black bar top. Pulling the phone away as he goes silent, the screen flashes 'call ended.' He hung up on me—again.

Fucker.

Every time I hear from him, it's a random phone call with the same question. So far each one's ended with me forced to give him the same reply and him hanging up without a word.

If Niko weren't my cousin's best friend and personal guard, I wouldn't have started searching for his sister in the first place. Now it's like an addiction. My own twisted drive is pushing me to hunt down and discover a woman who's been kidnapped since she was merely a child. This world's a fucked-up place to do that to a kid, that's for sure.

It's not even my damn department. I'm a *cop*, and not just your run-of-the-mill-parking-ticket-writer either. I'm undercover. I bust perps like Niko and the rest of my family, happily turning them over to the Feds. Hell, I almost was a Fed—and would still love to be—had it not been for my father popping up a while back, calling me out of the blue.

I've purposely distanced myself from that part of my family to prove that I'm nothing like that bloodline. I'm not *Mafia,* and I'm *not* a Masterson. Just to drive it in deeper that I'm different and I'll never belong to that side of my family, my last name's Masters.

Fuck. They've even got me speaking Russian now. I've *never* spoken Russian. I studied it along with the country my first year in college, and I was hooked.

I fell in love with the language at a young age, hearing my father speak it when I was a child. That only happened on the rare occasion he gave us a call, though, and I was lucky to catch him on the phone with my mom. The calls were never for me, only to speak to her. It used to kill me inside, but I grew to accept it. Mafia men are hard; they preach family, but it's never true. The life always overtakes everything, and most of them end up losing their families and the people they're closest to.

"Another?" My nod's curt, and I'm interrupted by my damn cell vibrating again. Stupid thing is always going off. Shaking my head toward the fresh drink, I swipe over the screen.

"Yeah?"

"It's Exterminator," he grumbles immediately. He's an outlaw biker I've come in contact with a few times. Criminal down to his bones, but that's beside the point, I need information.

"Did you find anything?"

Finally, he's called me back. I've been waiting for this guy to get back to me about another possible lead on Natasha. His motorcycle club went into Mexico for me, searching over a massive-sized cartel compound a few years back. They returned with nothing but a useless maid. To say I was disappointed is an understatement, and Niko was beyond furious it's taken so long.

I swear if my chief gets wind of me doing all this shit, my ass will be toast. I still can't believe that I initially agreed in the first place. I'm not supposed to get wrapped up in cases outside of the department. It's against protocol.

"No. Just another dead end."

"Fuck my life. Okay. Your money's been transferred already."

This time it's me hanging up and tossing the device onto the counter top. It feels like I'm back to square one each time I hit a dead lead, and it's costing a goddamn mint to head up the search for her. Where could these kidnappers be hiding this woman? Is she even alive at this point? I know she's most likely lost in the sex trade; it's discouraging and motivating at the same time. I couldn't let my own sister drown in that filth of a life—if I had a sister, that is.

My father's been funding this little venture. He thinks it'll win back his nephews. I, on the other hand, know he's a fool and should just stay the hell out of my cousins' way. Instead, he attempts to meddle in their business, not used to being out of the loop and not in charge. He's an idiot.

Yep, that's right. I'm an officer of the law, and my father's the previously pushed out, King of the Russian Bratva. It's ironic how life plays out sometimes.

Some may wonder why I'm not busy filling the role as King now, but I've never been in that lifestyle. I wouldn't know much about being a criminal, besides what I've learned as a peace officer. I've always veered in the opposite direction, especially seeing how paranoid my mom was while I was growing up.

My father stayed in Russia most of my life, so I grew up alone with my mom. She worked while raising me and we lived a fairly simple life. It wasn't until I was a little older that I learned exactly what my family was about.

I didn't know much about my cousins; Tate aka Tatkiv 'Knees' Masterson and Viktor 'The Cleaner' Masterson, until these recent years. They were the proclaimed Princes of the Russian empires since I was lucky enough to be hidden away. It was time for them to rightfully take their places at the head of the Russkaya Mafiya and Bratva but ran into some issues with their father, Gizya. He's my uncle—my father's brother—and as corrupt as the man himself. They're definitely related, that's for sure.

I helped make Gizya disappear without Viktor sinking him to the bottom of a lake or Tate beating him to death with a bat. You'd swear my cousin played professional baseball with the way that man can swing a bat at someone. Anyhow, I stepped in to offer them my assistance. I was shocked that they trusted me so easily, but they wrote it off as me being family.

Only the three of us know what really happened to Gizya and it has to stay that way.

That little experience forged a bond with two men I had no idea were so much like myself. They could be my own brothers, that's how at ease I always feel when I'm around them. I was also a little freaked with how much we all look alike. Even with me pushing away from the Mafiya, there's no doubt, by looking at me, where I come from and who my family is.

I've always known I was of Russian descent, but around those two, there's no question left in my mind. My hair's a bit lighter; I'm scruffier and covered in tattoos. Tate and Viktor have their fair share of ink, but my neck, hands, fingers, and calves are all done, whereas theirs aren't. The three of us have hazel colored eyes, a trait passed down by our fathers, and we all stand with the same build—muscular, but lean. According to my father, it's the frame of the perfect Russian leader.

He'd contacted me years back, needing my assistance. Niko's wife, Sabrina, had been taken against her will during Viktor's wedding, of all places. No one would expect anything like that to happen since the place was crawling with Russian soldiers and various men working security. I did what I could to help at the time. Granted, I wasn't as invested as I am now or I probably would've found Sabrina even quicker than I had.

I'm fairly certain her abduction was by the same people who stole Niko's sister when he was a child. Usually, that sort's all interconnected when it comes to the sex trade. Everyone knows one another in the business; it's almost like being a regular at a bar. Only it's not as simple as a friendly customer at the local drinking hole. It's a sick, fucked-up fetish, created by men wanting to control and abuse women.

With my newest idea gone to shit, looks like I may need to pack up and head to Houston. A buddy of mine I went to the academy with just so happens to be a Morelli. His gramps runs the Italian side of things in Chicago. I don't know what else to do. I've been searching for this woman for five years now.

I know—five years.

Huffing out a breath, I dial my father next.

"Da?"

"It's me."

"Moy sin!" My son, he greets.

"Da. I have business in Texas."

"I'll send my jet, nine p.m."

"Spaseeba."

"'Tis nothing. How are you, sin?"

"I'll call you if I hear anything."

I'm not calling to exchange pleasantries. I don't care how he is, and he doesn't need to know how I am. This is strictly business.

"Right." He finishes, and I hang up again.

Stupid phone.

"Another drink?" The older bar owner offers, staring at my still-full vodka he'd placed before me earlier.

"No thanks, cash me out."

Handing him two tens, I get to my feet, stuffing my cell in my pocket and grab my keys to my blacked-out Jeep Wrangler. It's pretty badass, jacked up on a seven-inch lift with some chunky thirty-sevens and custom rims. It's the one thing I spend money on to treat myself. "We're good," I say loudly and wave him off, so he keeps the change. It's not much—I'm Russian, so I like expensive vodka.

"Thanks."

He places the tip in one of the jars lining the bar, and I head out. The drive to my apartment doesn't take long thankfully, so I scoop up my ready-made duffle. I swiftly trade out my attire and lock my apartment up tight. It's nothing special, but it gets me by when I'm not busy on a case.

Flying in my father's jet and then meeting the Morelli family, I need to reek of business opportunities. One thing I'm good at, with being undercover, is adapting to different situations. Straightening my custom-tailored suit my father sent for my academy graduation years ago, I load back into my Jeep and head toward the airport.

The lady comes over the speaker as I hit the UConnect button. "Say call or options."

"Call."

"Who would you like to call?"

"Call Bax." That's the code name I have in here for my chief, and if I ever have to speak to him when the heat's on or if someone else checks out his number and doesn't use that name, he knows.

"Calling Bax."

It rings twice before he gruffly answers, "Bax here."

"Chief."

"Masters."

"I wanted to let you know I'm headed out of town."

"You're on vacation; you don't have to let me know if you're going out of town," he grumbles, and I huff.

"No, I'm on paid suspension until the Johnson case is over with."

"It's just the typical mumbo jumbo while the case is filed away. You have nothing to worry about; you followed protocol."

"I shot five people."

"They were criminals."

I can almost see his shrug as the words leave him. I know he'd be sitting behind his large, old oak desk, moving his shoulders like it's whatever. I've worked for him for six years now; we're used to each other.

"I'm leaving; don't want you to think I'm pulling a runner."

He starts chuckling. "Noted. Go have some fun Masters, you work too much."

"Says the man in charge of my schedule," I retort, and he laughs again.

"Safe travels and all that."

"Later, Chief." The UConnect beeps and turns off as he hangs up.

There's no reason to tailgate me

when I'm doing 50 in a 35.

And those flashing lights on the

top of your car look ridiculous.

-Funny Meme

Driving another ten minutes, I make it to the small private airport out in the middle of nowhere, it seems. My father's jet's already waiting for me. He said nine, yet it's 8:40. He must have sent it as soon as we hung up. He knows I'm an ass about timing too.

Perfect. I'm the type to be early everywhere I go. Fifteen minutes early to me is being on time; anything later is running late. Same way my boss thinks.

Stopping beside the stairs leading up to the plane, I'm greeted by the usual copilot.

"Good evening, Mr. Masters."

"Hello Trey, thanks for stopping by."

"No problem, sir. Are we taking the Jeep or parking it?"

"I'd like to bring it unless my father lined up a vehicle for me?"

"Yes, I uh, believe he has reserved you a car."

Staring into his guilty, coffee-colored brown eyes, I ask the million-dollar question, "What kind?"

"Most likely a Lamborghini."

"Jesus fuck, I'm supposed to blend in."

"He may have also requested it to be black or lime green, whichever the dealership has on hand, top of the line of course."

"I'm guessing he gave you instructions and had you line it up?"

He nods.

"Anyway, we can call them back and get a regular pickup truck or SUV?"

"No, I apologize, but he's already purchased it."

"I told him the last time to stop buying the damn cars; I'm fine with a rental."

"You totaled the last Mercedes."

"I was being chased down by Romanian thugs; I drive my Jeep just fine without wrecking it."

"Of course. Shall I have your Jeep parked?"

"Yeah, that'll work since I may be coming home with another car. I wish he'd stop buying me shit."

He grins. "It could be worse. I drive a Ford Fiesta."

"Maybe I'll tip you with a Lamborghini then."

"That sounds pretty fair to me." His smile grows wide, and I hand him my keys, grabbing my duffel.

"Thanks, Trey."

"No problem, Mr. Masters. If I may say so, you're looking quite the part today, sir."

Briefly, I glance down at the tailored suit. It fits me like a glove, accenting my muscles and trimmed waist. Drink Russian, shop Italian, and kiss French they say. Whoever 'they' is, clearly knows what they're talking about when it comes to that.

"I'm still a cop."

"You don't appear it in an Armani riding on a private plane."

"Touché," I respond and climb the stairs.

I'm pretty sure I got a hard-on the first time I rode in this plane. It's the quintessence of luxury. I've never thought of myself being materialistic in the slightest, but shit if I'm not spoiled by flying like this now. I'll never look at another plane the same way again.

"Welcome, Mr. Masters," the pilot greets as I enter the cabin.

"Hey."

"Where are we headed, Houston Hobby?"

"That'll work. Thanks."

He nods and disappears behind a door.

The beautiful stewardess comes out of the back, greeting me with a bright smile.

"Hello, Beau! I was excited to hear we were coming to pick you up."

"Oh yeah?" I grin at the pretty redhead.

"Yep! You're my favorite frequent flyer."

"Nice."

"Where are we taking you today?"

"I need to stop in Houston."

"This is why you're my favorite. I'll be able to do some serious shopping."

"Sounds like a plan." Winking, I take a seat on one of the rich, cherry-colored leather seats, buckling myself in until we're in the air and I can chill on the couch.

Trey comes through the door after a few minutes. "All set. I had a car service pick up your vehicle. They'll have it detailed and ready for pickup by the time you're back."

"Thanks, man."

"You're welcome. Enjoy the flight," he says and disappears behind the same door as the pilot.

"Are you thirsty or hungry, Beau?" The stewardess, Sue, asks, buckling in next to me for lift-off.

"I already ate, but I could go for some lemon water."

"Would you like some mint in it as well?" she asks, genuinely wanting to make me happy.

"Yeah, I'll try it. You got me hooked on the lemon water, so I'm up to try your other inventions," I reply, and she giggles as the plane ascends. Another perk about flying privately, we don't have to wait to take off and land as long as commercial flights do.

The plane touches down, and sure as shit, there's a bright, lime green Lambo waiting for me next to where the plane stops. It's completely obnoxious, screaming spoiled rich boy. It's exactly what I need, even if it's the exact opposite of who I really am.

"Your hotel and car info, sir." Trey pops the few papers in my hand as I stand, along with the key code to one of Houston's Elite hotel penthouses. He was busy doing more than helping the pilot it looks like. No matter how many times this happens, I'll never get used to it.

"Thanks, man, and I mean it about the car."

His smile is blinding at hearing me speak about giving him the Lamborghini again. I'm glad he's excited; my father will be livid — at me and not him, so it works out for all of us.

With a quick nod to the few staff, I descend the stairs, getting off the plane and toss my overnight bag into the passenger seat of the sporty green deathtrap.

"Have fun, Beau!" the cute stewardess calls from the plane.

I send her a brief wave as I open the driver's door and sink into the custom leather seats. *Fun, huh. I'll be lucky if I don't wind up shot anywhere.* Syncing my phone to the car, I dial my buddy. It rings once before he picks up.

"Has Hell frozen over?" He chuckles, skipping the hello.

"Mo!" I reply good-naturedly. "You missed me that much, eh?"

"I hear from you like every two years; you don't give me much of an option."

"Duty, man; the chief always has me busting my ass."

"You say that every time and I'll reply like I always do. You should quit the underpaid headache and come work privately for my family."

"Yeah, yeah. I'd hate to put you out of a job, 'cause you know once they see me work, they'll put you out on your ass."

His booming laugh flows over the speakers, causing me to chuckle as well.

"Okay, enough bullshitting, Masters; what's really going on?"

"I was hoping you'd be home so I could stop by?"

"Here? You're in Texas?"

"Yup, I'm headed toward the Woodlands as we speak."

"Well shit, come on over. I'll tell the gate to let you in. What are you driving this time?"

"Just some shitty Lambo."

His laugh is loud again as he ribs me. "Spoiled fucking rich boy, who knew! I don't know how you ended up in the academy in the first place."

"Shit happens—same story, different day. You know how that is."

"I do. All right Masters, see you in a few."

"Later, Mo."

With the last name Morelli and its crime association, he always had everyone call him 'Mo,' and it sorta stuck with me throughout the years. He knows a little bit about me, but not much. He's aware that I was slotted for the FBI, but when I went to the UK for my father, they discovered who I was related to.

Things changed with the Federal Bureau of Investigation from that point on. I was no longer a perspective asset to the company, but more of a hired undercover informant used to bust my own mafiya-born family. Once I heard their plans, I bowed out. I'm cold, but most of my family doesn't deserve to go down for the past generations' sick actions. My cousins, Tate and Viktor and their families, would've been affected and I couldn't do that to them.

They've kept my bloodline confidential, but I also know that they like to keep tabs on me. Once I went undercover with my department and started busting multiple criminals, they backed off a touch. I guess they figured out that I was the real deal when it came to law enforcement and doing the right thing. I'm not the cop you buy off or manipulate; I'm the one that'll put you away for life or six feet under if necessary.

I'm not stupid, though. I know I have to watch my six for the rest of my life. Not only from the dickfaces I put away, but also with the justice system I serve. That's one reason why I'm shaky about these five thugs I recently put down. You never know when the justice system or society may turn it so it looks bad, and then boom—you're spun into an informant to save your ass from jail time. I refuse to be put on that path. I'll hit the road before I ever let that happen to me.

The world's so fucked up now anyhow, with the ridiculous protesting and cop killing that citizens are saying is justified. None of it's okay. I never thought I'd see the world turn like this; makes me think about relocating to an entirely different country. Not sure my mom would go for that, though, and I damn sure wouldn't leave her here alone with the shit storm happening.

I pass by the Woodlands until I arrive just to the north. It's a beautiful area, and the area where Mo's family lives is surrounded by trees and green. One thing I love about it is the seclusion. You'd never know that there's a twenty-million-dollar mansion right in the middle of it all and down the road from the bustling city of Houston. It's a prime location for a mob boss to have a home.

They use this house as a winter home when they're not traveling outside the country. I can't blame them; Chicago at that time of year is cold enough to make you want to slit your own throat.

It reminds me of Russia. Visiting is cool, but living there? Fuck no, my California ass would turn into a Popsicle.

Veering left, I stop at an enormous black iron gate. The property's surrounded by trees, shrubs, and a massive brick privacy fence. Inside the barrier, the grounds are always kept up by various workers and there's a team of guards on constant lookout.

With all the precautions the Morellis take to protect themselves, it tells me that Mo must think highly of me for his family to allow me into their homes. I've been invited to the

Chicago house several times; I know the FBI would be salivating at that aspect if they found out.

It's not every day that you find an actual peace officer that's been born into the Russian Mafiya and has an in with the Italian Mafia as well. If the feds looked deep enough, they'd also discover that my boy, Finn O'Kassidy, is Irish mob. It seems like the more I attempt to distance myself from my roots, the more I'm surrounded by people *like* my own family.

Is he drunk or dodging potholes?

-Officers everywhere

"Sir?" A lanky built Italian pops his head out of a minuscule-sized tan brick building next to the call box.

"Beau Masters," I reply, accustomed to the protocol to enter the estate.

"ID."

I place my driver's license in his palm and wait. He swipes it under a black light and then types the number into a small laptop. Once he's finished, he hands it back to me and opens the gate.

"Pull straight to the main house and enjoy your visit."

"Thanks." I know better than to stop along the way and poke my nose in their business. I'm here for a favor, not to piss in anyone's Cheerios.

It takes me about five minutes of following the small road through the trees to reach the ginormous mansion of an estate. It's surrounded by dozens of bright pink bougainvilleas and deep green grass, the colors extra bright against the white exterior. What is it with rich people and the color white, anyhow?

The obnoxious green monster I'm driving stands out like a sore thumb against everything. My father claims the best way to go unnoticed is to be obscenely obvious. I don't agree with his methods, but he's the career criminal, not me.

Parking the green goblin, I make my way to the front door and stare. There's a ten-foot-tall glass water feature on the porch next to a beautiful variety of flowers. Every time I'm here, I swear it's my favorite thing about the place until I go inside and find a million other amazing things to proclaim as my top pick.

Mo opens the door wearing an expensive suit and friendly smile. "Masters! There's your ugly mug."

Chuckling, we do a man hug, and I step inside.

"What's good, Mo?"

His mocha-colored irises twinkle, with his jovial mood. "Staying busy like you. I have to admit; I was surprised to hear from you. Let's sit in the bar."

"You want to waste your good liquor on me, I won't complain." Grinning, I follow him through the sitting area toward an eloquently decorated bar. "Is your grandfather around?"

"Not today, but if this is business, I may be the one you want to speak to anyhow."

He pours vodka for me, and a Courvoisier for him then takes the seat next to mine at the round cocktail table. The bar has about a dozen small tables with two, oversized comfortable chairs at each. There's additional seating from rich, leather-covered couches placed tastefully around the room.

"I appreciate you letting me stop by and visit."

"As long as you leave the badge outside, you're always welcome here or in Chicago."

"Thank you; I appreciate the hospitality. I still wish you would've gone to the station with me; you would've made a half-assed decent partner."

"I told you, my being in the academy wasn't about becoming an officer. I was sent there as a punishment from my familia."

"I know, man; you just fit in really well."

He nods, sipping the strong amber liquid.

"Anyway, I've been keeping busy with a family matter."

"Non-work related?"

"No one knows about it besides my family and some bikers that've been helping me out."

"Bikers, Masters? Holy shit, have you flipped?"

"No. I still uphold the law. This has been a sort of a search and rescue thing, I guess you could call it. Years back, I received a phone call from my father. He needed me in the UK to help a woman that'd been taken. The woman's husband's sisters had all been stolen and sold off as well. There are three of them."

Taking a swig, I continue. "It's this huge underground sex-ring organization going on in Russia and other countries. They steal women and children, specific families and such, then auction them off to different countries. My cousins have found entire shipment containers full of women being transported. The conditions and treatments are sickening; the psychological damage is horrendous."

Pausing, I wait for him to be outraged, but he sits quietly like it's no surprise.

"You...umm...you already know all this, don't you?"

Swallowing, he nods silently, not incriminating himself. He knows I'm a cop. I wasn't checked for a wire, and he has every right to be cautious. I do the only thing I can think of to redeem myself and his trust that he's obviously questioning at the moment.

Remaining quiet myself, I stand and show him my palms. Then I peel off my shoes, one by one, handing them to him. He inspects each one carefully, and then I loosen my tie. I remove my jacket, unbutton my shirt and place them all on my chair. I spin in a slow circle with my arms out, so he can get a good look at me.

"Put them all inside the beer cooler," he responds and nods toward the bar. "Pants too."

Heading to the bar, I find the beer cooler, slide the top open, and shuck my pants off. I neatly fold my clothes and set them in a clean, clear plastic box. It's almost like it was there for this specific reason alone.

It probably is. I'm a dumbass.

"Underwear, good?" I call.

"Let's talk."

Striding back over to the table, I feel almost as if I'm in trouble. I'm stuck in my underwear, inside the home of one of the leaders of the Italian Mafia. I should write a book about the crazy shit I go through. Maybe when I retire.

Plopping down in the seat, I take a large gulp of my vodka to warm me. "We good now?"

"Yep, you've been hitting the gym." He nods to my torso.

"I have to man; crooks like to run," I reply, and he snickers, finally relaxed again.

"Tell me some more about your problem."

"Okay. So, one of those shipments that showed up, my cousin found his friend's sister in it. This is the same man whose wife I saved. Since then, I've been contracted to find his family. We're pretty sure his mother's long been dead. We think one of his sisters has been killed, but supposedly there's one more out there. I don't know why his family was targeted especially, but with his wife being abducted, it shows that he's clearly still on their radar."

"You haven't found her, I take it—the second sister?"

Shaking my head, I grumble, "No. I've been looking for five years."

He remits a grunt at hearing the time frame. "Five, Masters? You know what happens after that long—what the odds are?"

"Yes, I'm all too aware."

"Why have you kept going?"

"Because my father's stubborn and her brother's a psycho Russian who won't take no for an answer. He's out for her captor's blood, and it's less of a risk if I find the one responsible than if he does. He's Mafiya of course, and I don't want to draw attention to my family. I don't know where else to look. I've hired biker gangs to search for her; I've tapped surveillance systems of different crime organizations. I've done it all except ask for outside help, but I'm at a loss, man."

"And now you're asking?"

"Yes."

"Well, call me honored for you coming to my familia out of everyone for assistance. *But* you know these types of favors don't come for free."

"That's not an issue; my father is willing to pay. He only requires a cash number and a routing number."

"No, not that type of payment. I know exactly who your familia is. You should be the one running the Bratva right now. You're meant to be at the top — a Capo."

"No—"

He speaks over my interruption. "We'll want a favor based on your familia's Russian connections."

"I don't know if I can make that kind of a deal. I'm not their leader; I'm nothing to them."

"But obviously you're not nothing — you're something. If you're hunting down missing familia members and your father's funding the expenditure, you sell yourself short. It tells me that this venture is important enough to your familia to pay in favors."

"I see what you're saying. I'm sure if it's within reason, then my cousins will oblige."

"Yes." He chuckles. "Within reason, right."

"You know how I can find her?"

"I need any information you have, and I'll call my Uncle Luciano in Italy to see if she's anywhere in that area."

"Holy fuck, Sicilian mob Luciano Franchetti?" I gape.

He ignores the question. "Your familia knows there's a chance the girl is already dead, right?"

"I've told them that too. The last time I got a good lead on her was almost five years ago. I've gotten little clues here and there, but nothing solid. Her brother calls me on the first of every month, and I have to tell him each time that I have nothing. I saved his wife; now, he thinks I can save his whole family." My palm covers my face, rubbing over my cheeks and forehead in frustration.

"Shit."

"Yep."

"Okay, I'll talk to my grandfather and uncle about it, and I'll let you know what we find. Just send me an email with her information and any pictures you have. Leave search details out of the message; you know how it goes."

I nod. "Thanks. I don't have much on her though."

"Any other business on your plate?"

"No. Doubt I'd want to deal with anything else at this rate."

"Good, then get dressed so I can drive that badass Lamborghini you pulled up in."

"Does this go with the favors you were mentioning?"

"Nope, this goes with the part of being friends; we get to drive each other's cars."

"I see, and what kind of car do you drive again?"

"A Lincoln MKX."

"I'm pretty sure I'm getting the shafted end in this deal."

He smiles, grabbing my keys off the table as he stands. "Better hurry; you don't want to ride bitch in your boxer briefs. We may get pulled over with how fast I plan on going and think of how good you'd look booked in just your underwear."

"We better not get arrested!" I declare, quickly heading for my clothes. "And the next time you talk business, make the other guy take his watch off. You're slipping."

"This is why I should be the one paying you, not the police department."

Shrugging, I pull on my now freshly-chilled clothing and shoes. I'm too busy mentally preparing myself for my life to flash before my eyes with Mo's driving skills to be worried about my shitty paychecks from the PD. You don't become a cop to get rich, that's for damn sure. It's all about helping people, about being willing to protect and assist those in need while upholding the laws. I doubt making family favors would fall under any of that though.

Sapphire Knight

Clearly, I need more suits.

My phone vibrates with Morelli calling me, so I quickly press the green circle to answer. "You miss me already?" I ask right away, making him chuckle.

"Nice. And no, it takes more than a few days for me to get the blues, copper."

"Ha! Whatever, man."

"I have news."

My heart feels like it drops into my stomach with his words. So soon? I've been searching for years, yet within days he knows where Nikoli's sister is or could be? I'm glad, but at the same time, feel like a failure.

"Seriously? You've found her, already?"

"Well, not exactly. The boss in charge of everything is hard to pin down. Shit, it's hard to get a real first name even. Everyone we've spoken to calls him either 'The Master' or 'The Don.'"

"So, he's Italian after all," I mumble, my thoughts beginning to race. Or could he be Sicilian—old school mob, like Mo's uncle? Either way, it'll be a total pain in the ass; these guys never go down easily.

"Look, I can't talk much on the phone about any of it. We were able to locate the brother and get you an in. The only problem is, it's tonight in New York City."

"Damn, I don't know if my father's jet can get here soon enough to fly me up there by tonight."

"We have one I can send now. It'll probably take about three hours for the pilot to get to Cali. You won't be on time or early for the photographers, but you'll make it about midway through."

"What's going on that I'll be late to?"

"It's a charity ball, but with a very exclusive list. We called in a favor, but you were put on the list."

"Thank you; I owe you."

"Trust me; I know you do. We'll collect when the time's right. Grab a suit; it's strictly black-tie event. If you have any money in savings, bring it. You were made out to be a rich playboy that's been kept quiet to society. Grandfather really went out on a limb for you, being he thinks we're friends."

"We are friends. I let you drive my car, remember? And thank you."

"Don't thank me yet. You don't know the type of people you're about to be dealing with. I'll text you flight times. The Gala will have a room in your name for the night—it'll be bugged."

"The hell? Appreciate the heads-up."

"The Chicago Capo called in a favor. Trust me; they'll want whatever dirt they can get on you—or anyone else for that matter—to blackmail. Don't give anybody anything they can use down the way."

"Got it."

"You're still off work, right?"

"Yeah, I'm on paid leave for a while."

"Good; this may be a rabbit hole. Once you're in, you may need time to come out or decide what you want to do."

"What's that supposed to mean? You sound pretty damn cryptic."

"You'll see. This life isn't all butterflies and rainbows. You're about to get a fresh look firsthand at some shit going on in this world. Just leave your badge at the door and remember this is pro bono work, capisce?"

"I've been leaving my badge behind—more than I should—but I get it."

"Good. Watch your six, Masters; I'd hate to have some angry Russians on my back because you were messing with some twisted Italians."

"You had me thinking you were a badass for a minute; now you start showing your tail."

I hear him grumble to someone in the background for a second. "I have to go. I'll text you."

"Later, man," I reply, and he hangs up.

What the hell is it with people and just hanging up?

The charity is actually a real ball. As in women dressed in fancy, shimmering gowns and the men clad in expensive suits. If it weren't for the fact that it's full of the criminal underworld's elite, I'd stick out like a sore thumb with my tattoos and rougher-than-average features.

Once again, my father's suit he sent me, has come in handy. If they weren't so damn expensive, I'd invest in two, considering how often I'm expected to wear the damn things. I don't know how my cousin Viktor can sport one every day. Personally, I think they squish your nuts, but maybe I'm hung a little heavier than he is.

After circling the enormous room, I find myself at a long buffet table. It's decorated to the nines with a thick, beige fabric tablecloth and fancy flower arrangements centered every few feet down the entire length. Of course, the finger foods they're offering aren't the good kind. I'd kill for some spicy chicken wings right about now. Traveling on Morelli's jet, the crew wasn't as hospitable as my father's. Sue would've offered to make me a meal or a snack. Not even a bottle of water was presented, and now I'm starving.

Reaching for some toasted almonds rolled in sugar, a young lady catches my eye. I'd noticed her when I first entered the room, but she was carted away too quickly for me to get a good look. I can see her clearly from this angle, and the first thing I notice is how malnourished she is. Maybe anorexia? She could be a model attending these events for God only knows why. That'd explain it.

She places a few petite chocolate tarts on a small china plate, dutifully carrying it back to an older man. His hair's black with bits of silver creeping in, hinting at his true age. His barely-wrinkled skin and the expensive suit have him reeking of money. He's probably ten years older than he first appears thanks to Botox and facials. I could never do that to my face; I like to think I'm a bit too manly for that shit.

He gripes something to her in Italian, clearly irritated. When he lifts his head, his gaze meets mine, his features relaxing and schooling his expression immediately. His mask is fully in place, and how fitting, with his overly-stretched forehead.

Not one to be caught openly staring, my eyes quickly drop to the bowl of nuts and the tiny dessert dishes next to it.

It'd be so much more convenient to grab a handful and eat them, but I have to appear like I belong amongst these people.

Who the hell are they all anyhow?

I've searched the databases many times and haven't seen three-fourths of them in the criminal logs or on TV. They're obviously extremely wealthy, but how has the justice system never picked them up? I can tell they're criminals just by the way the men all watch each other like hawks — waiting to be stabbed in the back — and how they control their women.

"She's a peach, hmm?"

I'm startled out of my thoughts by the man I'd previously been observing.

"Excuse me?" I reply, and he sends me a wolfish smile. He's a shark; my gut can feel it already.

"Sasha." He nods to the frail woman, whose beauty would make everyone around jealous if her cheeks weren't so damn sunken in.

"Oh, what about her?"

"Tell me, do you like sweets?" He asks in with a heavy Italian accent, gesturing toward the chocolate tarts, his question confusing me.

"Sweets? Yeah, I have my favorites." I shrug him off, the hairs on the back of my neck standing up. Something's not right. This is the weirdest fucking conversation. Is he trying to hit on me?

"Sasha tastes as good as a homemade cannoli, so creamy. Just like licking the juiciest of peaches."

I have no clue what to even say to that. If it were my woman I wouldn't be bragging about her flavor to another man, and if anyone spoke about her like that, I'd put them through a wall.

"Or you prefer men?" His eyebrow shoots up, as he takes a drink of amber liquor nearly causing me to choke with his question.

"No, women only."

"Then you must be looking forward to the festivities later! I know I am." He winks, wearing a devilish smile. There's nothing friendly about it. He reminds me of a snake— a poisonous one—and up to no good.

"Yes, of course," I smirk back easily, completely lost on what the hell he's talking about but not willing to admit that to him.

"No worries, we're about to get rid of the wives, and it'll begin shortly. Sasha won't be available tonight, but there are plenty others like her."

Nodding, she approaches us, still holding the plate.

The man glares at her. "I told you to dump that. Get me another drink."

Her eyes dart to his feet. "Yes, Mr. Capelloni."

"I told you, call me Yema at these."

She takes his glass and rushes off toward the bar, leaving me alone once again with the strange guy. *Yema Capelloni.* I need to store that name away and run a check on it later. Yema watches me gaze after her, his smile growing with ideas.

"You want her?"

"She's not your wife?" His laugh is loud at my question, drawing the eyes of a few dancing couples in our direction.

"No, you really have been kept locked up tight, haven't you?" He chuckles, his laugh beginning to grate on my nerves.

"You know who I am?"

"Oh yes, of course. I know everyone in here, especially those with the most money. They all have no idea who you are though, and it's killing them. I love it." He claps me on my bicep lightly, acting as if we're good friends, and fuck if I don't want to punch him in his throat. My gut tells me he's nowhere close to being a friend. It's a ruse, a show in front of all these other people.

Who in the hell did Morelli's grandfather make me out to be? Rich playboy, but nothing special I thought. This guy's over here treating me like I'm his number-one customer, and I don't know what the hell he's even selling.

"Call me Yema, all my friends do, and I'll see if I can put Sasha up at the next one for you."

"When would that be again?"

"Next Friday. I'll make sure you're on the list," he says matter-a-factly and does a motion with his hand.

The music quiets and an old, white-haired lady in a fancy, navy blue ball gown steps before the crowd. A security guard hands her a small microphone, which she immediately brings to her mouth.

"Ladies and gentlemen, what a fantastic evening!" She smiles, and the guests clap softly, nodding like she's the queen bee. Her shrewd gaze shoots around the crowd, waiting for everyone's attention.

"We were able to raise five point two million dollars tonight benefitting the downtown art gala. I'd call it a success!" They all clap again, and I suppress the urge to roll my eyes. They're a bunch of stuffy asses dressed in double-digit outfits, worried about raising money. If they'd skipped all of this and wore a pair of jeans and tennis shoes, they'd be able to donate so much more. If it's really being donated that is.

"As much as I dislike the night fizzling to an end, it's time we turn in for our beauty sleep and allow our strapping beaus some time to visit. Thank you, thank you all for a marvelous evening." She finishes and hands the microphone to the guard.

All the wives kiss their husbands goodnight and head to say goodbye to the old woman. Yema leans toward me.

"They will be having cigars on the roof while we set up downstairs if you'd like to join them."

"Sounds good, thanks." I nod, not interested in the slightest to smoke. But I'll play along and get ready for whatever's going on downstairs. I wish Morelli would've at least clued my ass in on the events.

The guards escort the wives to the parking garage to— I'm assuming—the limos I saw when I first arrived. Everyone, including the press and possibly the cops out on the street, will see the limos pull off but never know that it's only the wives in them. Perfect alibi for whatever's about to take place I'm assuming. Smart. I'd have never thought twice about it either, had I not been inside and able to watch them split up. I'll have to put this in my future reports for possible scenarios with high profile criminals down the road.

The suits all shuffle toward another set of elevators headed to the top. I beeline my way to the restrooms, ready to hide out for a few minutes and see what I can scope out with everyone out of here. I'll get nowhere if I go up on the roof. It'll be a bunch of rich fuckers measuring their dick size, not talking about anything useful.

I need to find the hushed conversations, more than likely taking place in quiet whispers along hallways and in dark corners. The way Yema talks, I have a suspicion he's either who I need, or he knows the person I'm after.

Let the games begin...

I dip inside the restroom and pull my phone out. I want to be ready to record in case anyone decides to stop in and do some business. One positive attribute to these gatherings is the bathroom's so clean you could probably eat off the floor and be okay. I'm not trying it, but I don't think twice about planting my ass on a chair in the small sitting area.

A few younger guys bustle in without their jackets, rolling up their sleeves, heading for the sinks and I eavesdrop.

"I can't wait to see what he has for us this week," the first says with a British accent, turning on the water to wash his hands. I hit 'record' and place the phone into my breast pocket.

The other guy chuckles, turning on his own sink. He uses the water to fix any hairs that've gone astray. "Last week's load was prime."

"Capelloni says he can do better than Rishi."

"That's because Rishi Ah Mad picks up anything off the street, Maximillian. Capelloni however, only keeps the best with him."

"I hope you're right. My bank account's filling up, and I need to spend some bloody money."

They turn my way, drying their hands and the British one grins. "Too much to drink, lad?"

"Yeah, never can tell a woman bartender no," I reply and they both chuckle.

"That's the truth!" the American one agrees, as they leave the bathroom.

That went over perfectly; they didn't even notice me until they'd already spoken. I wish they'd have given up some more information. On the plus side, I have another name to check out later.

Shedding my own jacket, I roll up my sleeves, exposing my tattooed forearms and tuck my phone in my back pocket rather than my jacket. If anyone attempts to swipe it, I'll easily feel it with the fitted dress slacks, and it's convenient enough if I need it, I have it.

I toss my suit jacket over my shoulder and head back into the dimly-lit hallway. It's massive like the rest of the place and leads directly to the elevator and the two guys that were just in the bathroom. The floors are an expensive, shiny marble; the scones on the walls, no doubt costing a mint as well. The place reeks of wealth.

"You ready to spend some money?" The Brit named Maximillian, according to his friend, asks, and I nod.

I'm not really, but I'm guessing we're gambling. I'm not great, but I should be able to get by without draining my entire bank account. I know just enough to not come off as card counting or suspicious.

"Is it time?" I ask, playing along.

"Yep, let's head to the main event." The other guy replies as the elevator opens up and we all climb inside. "Tyson Blackwell." He holds his hand out to me.

"Good to meet you." I shake and turn away from him to the closed doors, not offering my name in return.

They don't need to know who I am, whoever that may be. I wish I'd been clued in. One thing in all of my undercover training I've learned not to do is volunteer any information. A man can own you if he has your name. With enough digging, he can find out damn near everything about you.

Keeping to myself, we ride down three floors before coming to a stop. The doors part and we're met with a room full of men, divided in the middle by a plain, black stage. The ceiling has multiple types of lights pointed toward the black surface, illuminating the path like it's a runway show.

The two men in the elevator scurry around me excitedly, pushing their way toward the front, but I hang back until I'm able to figure out what's really happening here. If shit goes down, I want to be able to jump in the elevator before all these criminals try to bail or put a bullet in me.

A beautiful—whom I'm guessing is Italian—woman with long, dark locks takes the stage. If she weren't in a sparkling red, floor-length gown, I'd think this was a private dance show. She brings a portable microphone to her chin with a sexy grin, and everyone quiets.

"Good evening gentlemen. I'm Victoria Franchetti, and I'll be your auctioneer for tonight's activity. Is everyone ready to see the fantastic selection we have tonight?"

The men cheer, causing Victoria's smile to grow. Another Franchetti and another name I need to commit to memory to check out.

"Great! Let's get the show started with our very own mouse! If innocent, librarians are your type, then get your pocket books ready!"

Music begins to float through the room softly. "Let's welcome Anna. She's our very own Italiano mouse! And be advised gentlemen, she takes orders *very* well. Her ideal night is only to meet your every need."

A petite, dark-haired woman walks out onto the stage, dressed up like a librarian, to play the part. She appears extremely young and nervous as she treads fully onto the stage, staring at her feet. As she gets closer, the men start yelling numbers, obnoxiously shouting higher amounts than the person next to him.

I'm guessing that I'm witnessing a bidding war amongst rich criminals, but for what? Prostitutes? Are these women even willing to be here?

Once Victoria calls out the highest-bid dollar amount, she scribbles down a name on a piece of paper, hands it to the girl and moves onto the next woman. As the night goes on, the women are auctioned off like cattle, and the men celebrate as if they've won the lottery, spending hundreds of thousands of dollars and slamming back too much booze.

After the fifth woman departs the stage, Yema approaches me. "You haven't found one that pleases you yet?"

I shrug, not responding directly. My eyes find Sasha tucked away behind him. She's like his shadow — an assistant, perhaps? She pleases me.

"Ah! You like blondes, then?"

I shrug again, not caring if I come off as rude. I'm here for Niko's sister. I haven't seen anyone remotely close to her description yet.

"I'll have to get some more blondes for you. Maybe Brazilian or is Russian more to your taste? Which do you like more?"

"Russian. Russian blondes," I mutter, watching Sasha's cheeks heat at my declaration. She's undeniably Russian. "And tall." Sasha's short, but Niko's sister would most likely be at least five foot eight or higher comparing to him and his other sister.

Yema chuckles. "Yes, I like Russian women myself, especially the ones that have already been broken in. I assure you, all the women here have been trained properly and will satisfy your every need. You want to cut them? Done. You like beating them? Done. You want to watch them with others? Done. You seek only your pleasure? Done. You ask, and you receive. They know what is expected of them."

I knew I wanted to hit this cockroach for a reason. I would never touch a female in any of those ways. If that's what's going on, these people are fucking sick.

"Why would I spend so much for a few hours or one night? I could get a hooker willing to do anything for the right price. Strip clubs are crawling with them. I snap, and they come running."

"I do not doubt you. This is not for one night only," he replies stiffly, searching for the right words in English like I've struck a nerve. "These are prime picked, broken in, disease free, and yours for as long as you wish. You pay the highest bidding price, and she's yours to keep. You will own her."

"And if I wanted this one?" I nod toward Sasha, my finger gesturing up and down, wishing it could actually touch her skin.

"Then I'll speak to my boss and have her ready for the auction next week. You can purchase her."

"You don't object?" I peer at her, but she remains quiet, and he laughs cruelly, sneering in her direction.

"She isn't allowed to speak. You do not own her yet. Have some fun tonight, and I'll make sure she's prepped for next Friday."

"What if I want her now? I don't like to wait." I'm supposed to be a rich playboy, so may as well play the part and see if I can get more information from him and possibly take her home with me to safety.

"You would have to pick another tonight, keep her for a week and then get Sasha at the next ball. You can kill the one you get tonight when you get bored or sell her to get some of your money back."

"I see." I'm furious, storming inside as I'm enlightened as to what's really happening tonight. I wish I could bid on them all, but there's no way. I've watched how much they've been going for; I don't have that kind of money.

There's nothing I can do tonight, except try to remember these men's faces and pray that there's a god kind enough to give them a little more time for me to find them as well. I wasn't cut out to be this type of a criminal, but being a cop right now doesn't sit well either. There's a special place in hell for these sorts of men, and I'd love to pull my forty-five out right now and send them on to their new home in hell. That's the mafiya in my blood coming forward, the urge to kill these men with no remorse.

Turning from him, I gaze toward the stage as a tall, lanky, dark-haired woman takes the stage. She's not my type, but I need information from her. If I had enough money, I'd buy them all after hearing his spiel on what is allowed to be done to them. This must be what Morelli meant by telling me to leave my badge at the door and remembering this is pro bono.

The men start shouting numbers that automatically trump my entire bank account and net worth. She goes quickly to an older man. She must be a special type to go so fast. It makes me sick inside knowing I can't buy them all and take them off to a better way of life.

Yema carts Sasha away and I swipe a rocks glass full of something strong off a passing server. She keeps on her path, passing the cocktails around to anyone needing a refill. I need the burn to help pull me from my dark thoughts of killing as many of these men in here as possible. The need to protect these women is clawing at me like a man fighting to breathe.

Chugging the liquor down, another woman comes on stage—this one curvier but still very thin. Whoever's in charge is no doubt starving them. This woman should have thicker thighs with her build. Sick fucking pigs. No doubt that's not the worst they've done to these beautiful creatures.

She's bid on and won by the British man, Maximillian, I'd come across in the bathroom. They push her off to the side quickly and call on a new name.

This one reminds me of an angel. Covered in bruises, with white hair, I can't hold myself back from shouting numbers, competing for the highest bid. An old fucker shouts one hundred thirty thousand dollars and the liquor kicks in on my empty stomach, egging me on further.

"One hundred seventy thousand dollars," leaves my mouth in no time, causing my stomach to churn at the imaginary number in my personal account.

There's no way I can pay for it. They'll hunt me down and slit my throat before I'm able to make any headway, let alone get to next Friday to save Sasha's fate as well. I'll run if I must to try and save at least one of them.

"Sir?"

Blinking, I shake the fuzziness the strong liquor's beginning to inflict. I've literally had two drinks since I've arrived. They have to be laced with something. Fuck, how am I going to explain this on my drug test and to the chief? What was in those glasses?

"Your name, sir? So I can mark her for pickup."

Clearing my throat, I reply loudly, "Masterson. She belongs to Masterson."

A collective gasp echoes through the crowd as I state my cousin's last name. No way in hell am I giving mine. My brain's fuzzy; no wonder these dicks spend so much money in here.

"Russians?" Is whispered several times amongst the men as Victoria's mouth visibly drops open, staring in shock.

"I thought they were out of the sex trade?" is mumbled around me and it sets in what this auction really is. I thought I knew, but I had no fucking clue just what this bidding war was funding exactly. Now I have my answer. And then the sickening fact that I just contributed to it with money I don't really have as well. No doubt my father will have to foot this bill.

Yema comes to stand beside me again, wearing a large, pleased smile. "Yes! Mr. Masterson has made his bid, now mark it and move on." He claps me on the back like we're pals, causing half the room's eyes to bug out at the gesture. Turning to me, he asks quietly, "How shall we bill you?"

"Send my tab to my father; he'll cover it. Make sure I get her next weekend." I gesture toward Sasha. "I want blondes, lots of them."

He chuckles, delighted. "You will have her, and I'll see about any others. I'm glad you found one that pleases you." Glancing at Sasha, I'm surprised to find her glaring daggers at the white-haired woman that I just bid on standing off to the side.

"You hear that, Sasha?" I speak to her directly, calling her attention back to me. "You're mine next, blondinka."

Her icy irises meet mine, flashing at me calling her blondie in her native tongue. She wants to say so much, I can tell, but she remains quiet. One glance at Yema and her shutters come down, her eyes void of the fire I just witnessed in them. I'm surprised to see any spark in her at all if they're all treated so badly by Yema and his boss.

Everyone turns back to the festivities, minus a few curious stares, still taking me in now that they know I hail from the infamous Russian crime family.

"Mr. Masterson, a word if you will." An old guy with grey hair and enough wrinkles he could be part chow approaches me.

My eyebrow hikes, waiting.

"I was under the impression your family had gotten out of these types of transactions."

Nosey fucker. I have absolutely no idea what to say to him about it. I'm not Tate or Viktor—they handle this sort of thing. I'm not a Big Boss; I'm merely their cousin who's been kept a giant secret from it all. It's mostly my own doing with my aversion to the entire lifestyle.

"I don't discuss business like this." The sneer radiates from me naturally, born with my father's blood coursing through my veins and the distaste for what's going on around me. If I could, I'd put a bullet in his forehead as well as the others. It's not logical though; they'd kill me before I made any leeway.

He clears his throat, almost appearing ashamed to have even approached me about it. "Of course, my apologies for bringing it up when we should clearly be celebrating. Let me give you my number. I go way back with Victor. We should catch up; I believe we could mutually benefit."

I'm assuming by his age he means my father and not my cousin and I'm guessing he has no clue that's my father he's talking about. Or does he?

"Great."

He hands me a card, which I tuck away immediately, not giving him the satisfaction of knowing that I care who he is. I do though. My palm's itching to pull the square cardstock back out to find out exactly who he is.

He shakes my hand and walks back over to—I'm assuming—his bodyguard. Others peer over at me, probably contemplating whether they should introduce themselves to me as well. I need as many names as possible, but deep down, I'm hoping they fuck off until next week, so I can catch my bearings and get a new plan going. This is not a goddamned meet and greet.

I could seriously kick Morelli's ass for not telling me what I was walking into tonight. Probably best he didn't, or I may have come with backup, or at least my cousins and that would've ended with guns blazing I'm sure.

I'm not so much worried that they know I'm related to the Russian Mafiya as I am with them finding out that I'm an undercover cop.

Promises, promises…

"You will be back?" A soft feminine voice asks from behind me, causing my gut to clench. Not with sickness but with lust at hearing the melodic sound.

Turning, I find Sasha in my shadow.

Her voice, coming from those lips. I think, staring at them, licking my own, and imagining what they must taste like. Damn it, why couldn't I have her tonight? Not have, I mean protect.

Fuck. What am I thinking? I have to stay on task—fuzzy headed or not.

"I swear it," I murmur, my voice husky from my thoughts of kissing her.

Her gaze drops to the floor as Yema steps beside me again.

"Was she speaking?" He gestures toward Sasha.

"She gasped." I flash him a cocky smirk. "My fault, I was telling her what I was planning to do to her next weekend. She couldn't help but be turned on. Just the response from her I wanted. She'll be perfect."

His brows raise, pleased to hear my answer that his little slave is making me happy, and in return, making him money.

I'm glad he seems to be buying the bullshit that I've been feeding him. I'm not sure how much longer it'll last before he realizes I'm making it all up. One thing is for certain, I have to come back for her. I'll borrow the money from my father if I have to, but I can't leave her fate in any of these pricks' hands.

"Let me introduce you to your new pet." Yema grins as if he's giving me a present.

"The sooner, the better."

He heads toward the side of the stage, Sasha following along with a glower painted on her lips. The other men still busily bidding on women step out of our path, giving us plenty of space.

"You know, I can sell them to you in bulk if you're happy with this one."

"Blondes in bulk? Would I get bulk pricing?" I feel like a fucking dog speaking the words.

Sasha scoffs. Yema misses it, but it's loud enough for me to catch it. She's so bland when it comes to him, but fiery when I show interest in other women. She doesn't even know me, yet she's already staking a claim? Why? Because I promised to come back?

"We can work out a deal." He nods, motioning for the woman I bought to come over to us.

She does as she's told and approaches us. As she nears, I can make out the bruises along her arms and legs. She's most likely anemic and hasn't been getting what she needs to prevent all the bruising. I can only imagine what kind of condition she's in underneath the cheap dress-thing she's got on.

As soon as we leave here, the first thing I'm doing is getting her something to eat and feeding her a few of my multi-vitamins. Who cares if they're the men's kind, these women are falsely advertised. Minimal money spent to make them look presentable enough to be sold. Maybe with some kindness, they'll give me the information I'm looking for.

"Shall I have someone take her up to your room?"

So they can most likely kill me now that the entire room knows I'm Russian? I love the idea of crawling in a comfy plush bed, but I'd rather sit in a car at the airport and wait for my father's jet than chance taking a bullet to the brain or a knife to the back.

"She can come with me now. I have a thing about hotels, even if they are suites." The lie slips from my lips easily, a little too easily in fact. It's one of the bad habits of this life. Lying successfully can save your ass in a pinch, but sometimes you do it, not realizing before it's already happened.

"Well then, enjoy your latest purchase, and I'll be sure you get on the list for next week. Do you have a card so that I can get in touch with you?"

"Not on me, I wasn't planning to do much business tonight."

"I see. No worries." He pulls a blank card with only a number scripted in black on one side from his breast pocket and hands it to me. "You can reach me directly. Thursday morning I'll have an address for you, and I'll see about setting a group off to the side for you. Please invite your familia if they're interested to get involved again."

"I look forward to it, and I'll pass along the invite." I nod, turning to gaze at the white-haired woman. "Do you have a name?"

She peers up at me through long lashes and sad eyes. "Whatever you wish to call me is my name."

So not only are they selling human beings but they're brainwashing them as well. I hope she can tell me something that will help in my search. I probably come off as a heartless bastard, which is a good way for Yema to think of me. If I hadn't already seen so much fucked up shit going on being undercover, I'd be a goddamn mess right now. Experience is keeping me grounded and alive at the moment, nothing else.

"What was it they called you up on the stage?"

"Trixie."

"That's your real name?"

She shrugs like she's unsure.

Fanfuckingtastic.

"Hmmm, you're not a Trixie. I'm going to call you Willow."

"Oh, I like that name." She smiles softly, and Yema scoffs, glaring down at her until her eyes hit the floor again.

"Yema, until next week," I interrupt, and he responds, shaking my hand and thanking me for my business.

I didn't just go shopping for fuck's sake. This is a person, not a new pair of shoes.

Wrapping my arm around Willow, I pull her close and start our trek to the elevator. "Come on, sweetheart." She comes willingly, riding up the few floors until we hit the parking garage.

"You're not going to hurt me, are you?" She finally breaks the silence once we're in my rented Cadillac CTS and she's securely buckled in.

"Why do you say that?"

"Because you have kind eyes. The others didn't look like yours; they didn't watch me like you do."

"You hold that thought, and we'll talk about it a little later. Right now I want you to finish that Gatorade." I gesture to the half full container of red liquid that I'd purchased after getting my rental.

"All of it?"

"Yep, every drop."

"Would it be okay if I saved some? I would like part of it tomorrow also."

Jesus fucking Christ, I swear I'm going to kill someone for this shit.

"No, you drink it all. I'll buy you a case of it for tomorrow if you would like."

She squeals happily, rushing to get the cap off so she can chug the still-cold beverage.

Afterward, she hums, pleased. "Thank you so much for being the one to buy me. I'll do whatever you wish, I promise."

"Good. We're going to get on my father's plane. It's waiting for us at the airport, and then we're leaving here as quickly as possible."

"Where will we go?"

"To Tennessee."

"Is that your home?"

"No. We're going to visit my cousins; they live there. I'm going to have one of their guards, Alexei keep you safe."

Undercover Intentions

"Oh." She says more quietly. "Is he a mean man?" she asks, nearly whispering the words. Her English is great; you'd barely be able to hear the Russian to her words if you weren't listening for it.

"No. No one will be unkind to you, Willow. That I promise *you*."

She lets out a relieved breath, sinking into the seat like she's able to finally let her body relax. And it makes me want to catch all of these fuckers even more. Before it was about finding Niko's sister. Now it's about rescuing these women and eventually handing over the perps to my cousins.

Our justice system could never punish them severely enough to atone for their sins. Tate and Viktor can. This is what Mo meant about me making up my decision how to go about things later down the road. He knew I'd feel this way, that a jail cell wasn't a strong enough punishment for these types of monsters I'm dealing with now.

'Me, Myself and I' by G-Eazy comes on the radio, so I turn it up. The music relaxes Willow further, and she's fast asleep by the time we reach the private airport where my father's jet's waiting on standby. I'd bet that liquid she drank was the only thing she'd had to eat or drink today, and that's why she was able to fall asleep. She'll never go back to a life like that again; I'll make sure of it.

The flight's a swift one. No stops on a private plane makes any trip hassle free. I don't think I've ever been so grateful for having a rich father with all the traveling I've

73

been doing. I appreciate him footing this bill; although I'm a little antsy about how he'll react to my Russian Mafiya declaration and sticking him with a huge tab. According to my mother, my father will help me no matter what I need; all I have to do is ask. I'm not the type to go requesting favors though. As far as I'm concerned, this is all to help out his family, and I'm the one doing the favors here.

"Where are we?" Willow mutters groggily as I help her get loaded into the waiting SUV. She yawns and stretches her thin limbs.

"We've made it to Tennessee. Now we're headed to my cousin Viktor's cabin. It's still a ways from here. It's not too long, but you can sleep some more if you'd like."

"You're not tired yet?"

"My head was fuzzy earlier, but I was able to nap a little on the plane. I'm used to sleeping odd amounts of time. I'll be okay to drive us."

"Okay." She nods, curling up toward the window once I close her door. She looks so soft and innocent sleeping against the door like that. No one would ever guess that she was just purchased from an underground sex-trade auction.

I get comfortable, adjusting the seat and mirrors to my liking and start on the drive to Viktor's, running over each face and name I can remember what feels like a million times to commit them to memory.

Strength does not come from

physical capacity. It comes from

an indomitable will.

-Gandhi

It's around three a.m. when my cousins arrive from their own flight. Tate's hammered, off bourbon if I had to guess, so he heads straight for a guest room without two words in passing. Viktor, his right-hand man Alexei, Tate's right-hand man Niko, and Viktor's wife Elaina's guard Spartak each take a seat around the kitchen table. Fatigue's written all over their features from the long day that they obviously had themselves.

"Sorry I had to flake out on you guys, but some shit came up."

They're always inviting me to different events, and somehow I never end up joining them for one reason or another. After a while, it's made me start to feel like a real dick for blowing them off.

"Clearly, you had important business keeping you," Viktor replies, easily accepting my excuse. He always does though; I think it's one of the main reasons why we get along so well. We both have busy lives, and we both easily accept it from the other.

Niko sits forward, drinking from the large Styrofoam cup that holds what smells like vanilla coffee. "Is this because of the chick sleeping on the couch?" he asks bluntly.

"Yes." I scrub my palm over my face, sighing. "I discovered a little more than what I was expecting tonight. The Morellis got me into an 'event' of sorts. I thought it was merely a stuffy charity function; turns out that late at night, it's an auction. Not just any kind of auction though. I bought the woman on the couch. I had to announce that I was part of the Russian Mafiya to the entire damn crowd to get them to let me have her. It was fun, I'll say that much. I thought we were going to be gunned down getting into the elevator."

Viktor's hand slams onto the tabletop. "Fuck. Not good."

"Nyet. Not good, Copper." Niko shakes his head, calling me by the nickname he's so cleverly dubbed me with. Being that I'm a cop and all, his creativeness is astounding sometimes. His serious gaze remains trained on a steak knife left on the table, waiting for me to continue, and the other two men remain quiet, listening to everything.

"I didn't have a choice. They doubted me, and in that instant my options were limited. Plus I had no way to pay for the girl, and you should've seen the scum that was salivating over them all. If I weren't on leave right now, I would've flashed my damn badge and called in for some backup or something. Hell, I doubt SWAT would've caught them all, there were so many people stuffed in that room."

"You're being punished for doing your cop job, not off on vacation. And what do you mean all? There were other women for sale in this place?" Niko's Russian accent's thick as he attempts to keep his cool. His words leave him in a rush, alternating between Russian and English as his eyes finally meet mine. There's anger brewing in their depths, so much going through his mind, no doubt about his kidnapped sister and if she could've been there tonight.

"Yes, there were a lot more."

"Usually the sales are smaller, only three or four women being sold and held in one location," Alexei interrupts. He may belong to the Bratva, but most of the time he thinks things over like a cop. I respect him and his choices. He's not careless like I've witnessed so many other criminals be, and he helps keep my cousins safe.

"I have no clue how many there actually were tonight. It seemed like they were being herded in and out like cattle. One by one, they trekked up onto the stage and then were sold within minutes." I nod toward the living room. "I grabbed her, Willow. But like I said, there were so many others. It killed me to leave and let it all happen like it did. I wanted to bring them all with me."

"You think my sister was there?" Niko peers at me, hopeful but wary all the same.

"I'm not one hundred percent sure, but there's a chance she could be. Anything's possible. You know that from finding your other sister. I did tell them my type was tall blonde women though, and they didn't show me any, just short women."

"She could have any color hair, who knows." He glowers, angry at the thought of her being trafficked into the sex trade.

"This wasn't the first occurrence, from my understanding. This seems to happen all the time, which is horrifying; but in this instance, it's good for us to find out more information. Attendees have to be invited and then placed on an approved list to even enter, and that goes for both events. There's the boring charity for all the wives to start the evening. Once that charade is over, the wives and drivers leave, so it looks like the event is over, and everyone went home. Then in the basement, all the men stay to drink and bid on 'prizes.' It's fucking sickening and yet genius all rolled into one."

"So how do we stop it?" Viktor mumbles, thinking out loud while tapping his fingers on the table. He's a smart man and no doubt he has a few scenarios running through his mind on the best way we should handle this.

"There's another charity function coming up. I'm supposedly already invited. The guy in charge is supposed to get me a group of blondes. He thinks I'm some spoiled manwhore spending my trust fund from my father."

"Shit, an entire group? Does he know who your father is?" Spartak asks, astonished.

"Yep, the guy told me he could get them in bulk. Spoke about it like I was at Sam's Club buying paper towels or some shit. Fucking sicko. And I'm not sure if he realized exactly who I am; another approached me too."

"Bastards!" Niko complains angrily.

"Were you able to find out who any of them are?" Alexei asks, on the same page as Viktor, working out what to do next.

"The guy I spoke to was called Yema."

Alexei's fingers pull at his stubble along his jaw as he ponders over the name. "Was there any mention of Luciano or Leopoldo Franchetti?"

Viktor's eyes grow wide as understanding hits him on where Alexei's going with this. "You think the UFC fight we were at in Chicago was a cover for the Franchettis? They would've had an alibi if the auction got busted, and if it didn't, then they were in town to handle business."

"Makes sense," Alexei agrees.

"Yes, briefly. Well, Morelli said he'd call his uncle to ask if he knew anything. He said Luciano. I asked if it was Franchetti, but he never confirmed my suspicion. I didn't hear the name Leopoldo at all, however. Do they have a brother named Yema? I think the guy I spoke to was the brother of whoever was in charge, but I'm pretty sure his last name was Capelloni unless that was bullshit too."

Viktor shakes his head. "No, he may have let you think he was the brother or some of their people may be saying that, but they'd never put themselves open to risk like that. Yema was probably just another soldier acting like he's more important than he really is. To someone new like you, for example, you think you're dealing with one of the bosses so if shit goes down, the real bosses stay safe and out of it. The lower guy takes the fall or in some cases, dies. The Franchettis are Sicilian royalty and never get busted for anything. They're always somehow in the clear when something goes down. This would be a prime example of how they pull it off."

Well shit! I thought I was making so much headway. I know what they're saying about the fall guy is true; I should have seen right through it with all my undercover training. Sasha had me distracted along with the drinks and then with them having the element of surprise. I won't be fooled so easily next time: I'll make sure of it.

"Then that makes the Morellis related to the Franchettis and part of the Sicilian side of things." I begin piecing it all together like a giant puzzle.

"Yes," Viktor confirms. "Capelloni sounds like one of the houses in New York. There's a chance that the families are working together and that's why it's so hard to peg anything concrete down on who's responsible."

"How's your relationship with them?"

"We haven't had too much of a ripple from them since we got out of the sex business. We practically gave it to them, and they stay out of our way when it comes to weapons. With us poking our noses in their auctions though, expect things to get a bit out of control. You definitely need to watch your back more, maybe keep one of the guards with you."

"I don't want the kind of attention on me that having a guard around will bring."

"They already know you're Russian. Think Beau; if you're the spoiled rich boy, doing whatever you want, and spending papa's money...Any father in this family would have protection on you to keep you alive. You'd look like less of a threat if you had one with you. No one knows that you're a badass underneath that suit."

I shrug, not thrilled with the idea but not ready to admit yet that he's most likely right.

"What do we do with the mouse?" Niko mumbles, interrupting.

My cousin glances over at me, showing me respect by letting me decide what we do.

"I was going to speak with you about Alexei keeping an eye on her. Would it be a problem?"

I assured Willow that they'd be nice and protect her. I probably should've asked my cousin before me spouting off those promises though. If push comes to shove, I can figure out a safe space but would prefer having my cousin's assistance.

Alexei protests quietly. "Me? We have plenty of other guards." Evidently, he's not too amused with the prospect of having babysitting duties and me so easily volunteering him for them.

"If you want her to stay here, I think it's a smart idea, and I agree." Viktor nods his approval.

He turns to his right hand. "Lexei can make her feel safe, which judging by the women we've already discovered from this underground sex trading, feeling safe will be very important for her. Now, let's all get some sleep, and we can discuss this further tomorrow. Once my brother has slept off some of his stupor, perhaps he'll have suggestions. I'm sure there's much more we need to hash out as well." Viktor stands, and we all copy him, pushing in our chairs.

"There is," I confirm. "I appreciate your help." Reaching out, I offer him my hand, grateful.

He shakes it, nodding to me and then ordering Alexei. "Lexei, carry her to your bed, she can sleep with you. She may be scared being around the other guards, and you have a private room."

"She hasn't even met me yet, and I have a small bed." The wrinkle on his forehead grows more prominent with his disgruntled frown.

Viktor remains silent, staring down his General, daring him to argue further with his orders.

"I'll put her against the wall, then I can watch her, and she won't fall out of the bed." He finally relents, satisfying his boss.

"I have a bed and a beautiful blonde printsyessa waiting for me; I'll see you all tomorrow." Viktor declares tiredly, and we all bid each other good night.

I head to the guest room I always use whenever I visit. The cabin was tiny the first time I came around, but with the family growing, Viktor and Elaina have expanded their home. It's more of a fancy compound now with everyone always around.

It's peaceful, and I find myself forgetting about the outside world when I'm here surrounded by my family. Funny, growing up, I never thought that I'd ever consider them as my 'family,' but they are. We're more alike than I'd care to admit sometimes. I've had time to make peace with it though, and it's comforting knowing I have someone else to turn to besides my mother.

Sleep overtakes my body nearly as soon as my head hits the pillow with dreams of a specific beauty filling my mind.

Morning comes far too quick for my liking, but I have work to do, so I man up and face the day. The hot shower feels fantastic against my skin as I try to scrub last night's filth off me. No matter how much soap I use, I can't stop thinking of those women in the building's basement.

Imagine your own daughter being taken from your home in the middle of the night. She's then tortured and raped until a certain age, or she reaches a submissive state then traipsed across a stage, where she's put on sale for some old sicko with a little girl fetish. That's what I think of when I have to look at these men's faces. Well, that and I also imagine gutting them for it.

"Breakfast?" Viktor's wife asks as I come into the kitchen, dressed in a fresh pair of jeans and T-shirt. Tate and I dress fairly the same; Viktor, however, always looks as if he's headed to a business meeting.

My cousin's at the table, thumbing through a copy of the *New York Times*. *The Chicago Tribune* rests folded in front of him as well. He's been busy already, no doubt looking for anything helpful in the society pages.

"Coffee would work."

She smiles my way as Viktor interrupts. "It's on the counter."

Elaina frowns toward her husband. "I can fix him a cup of coffee."

"He's our cousin, not a guest. Beau, help yourself. Our home is your home."

"Erm…thanks." It's too soon for all this conversation. I need some caffeine before I can function a hundred percent.

The door leading outside opens with Niko and a tired looking, hungover Tate coming in to join us.

"Hey guys, want some breakfast?" She tries again.

This time Viktor lays the paper down and shoots a glare at Elaina. I'm not fully awake yet, so it's harder to hold myself back and not laugh at them. I know she's doing it on purpose now to press Vik's buttons; she hates being ordered around. Men bigger than me won't think twice about obeying the King of the Bratva, but not her.

I've seen Elaina stand up to him many times over the years and yet neither of them learn, always squaring off about something, and then he carts her off to the bedroom. They'll eventually make their way back. She'll be wearing a bright smile, and he'll be less tense; happens every time it seems.

"No thanks; Bina cooked for me." Niko grins.

"Just coffee. If I eat, it's coming back up," Tate mumbles as he and Niko take a seat at the table. Elaina gestures me toward the table and starts pouring cups of coffee for all of us.

"Rough night, moy brat?" Viktor asks a little too loudly and joyful.

"Shut up. You know how much I drank."

The back door opens again, this time with Spartak ducking through it. He nods to everyone and heads for the coffeemaker. He obviously knows better than to let Elaina wait on him or even ask if he wants something.

"Anyone heard from Lexei yet?" Vik folds the newspapers in half and pushes them toward the middle of the table for anyone else that may be interested.

"I heard him yelling when I was outside. I think the girl Beau brought with him was having a nightmare or something. It sounded like he was trying to wake her up," Spartak responds as he takes a seat across from me.

Fuck. I thought he'd be able to handle her. Maybe I should've kept her with me instead. "I'll go check on her." I start to stand, and the guys all look at me like I'm nuts.

"You can't do that," Niko declares.

"I probably should; I'm responsible for her."

Viktor shakes his head, "Not anymore, you're not. Alexei can handle her. If he needs help, he'll let us know. Until then, let him take care of her; it's his job. Give him a little time before you try to interfere. He needs to get her to trust him."

"You're sure? I don't want her anymore freaked out. You should've seen how uptight she was when we left the gala and I told her that another man would be watching out for her."

"I can imagine. The abducted women we'd found in the crate awhile back were so messed up. It's taken time and

86

trust for Nikoli's sister and the other captives to come around. Lexei knows, and will comfort her if she needs it."

My cousin's reassurance helps a little, reminding me that he and his men have dealt with this sort of thing before. Saving and rehabilitating women who were kidnapped and forced into the sex trade has sort of become their mission, aside from their not-so-savory businesses. Clearly, our genes can't be all bad if we each attempt to help people in some ways. It was our fathers who were the really bad ones, knee deep in prostitution and heroin distribution.

"You brought a woman home?" Tate perks up, his bloodshot gaze meeting mine. Nodding, I fill him in on what I told everyone last night, along with any other details I may have missed last night in my tired state. Tate has a wife, Emily, and he's fiercely protective of her. I swear that runs in our family as well—the Alpha gene.

Elaina overhears everything we go over, getting angrier by the minute. I know she must be bursting inside to be able to say her piece. Viktor will be getting an earful from her later, that's for sure. Until then, she'll remain quiet, as is expected of her being the King of the Bratva's wife. This is business and one thing Viktor's made very clear to her over time, is that it's no place for her when he's speaking with his men.

Staying here occasionally has made me privy to seeing them push and pull to find their balance. She respects him enough to wait until they're behind closed doors to voice her thoughts and suggestions. He returns that respect by listening and taking her advice when it fits with whatever's going on. It's taken patience and a few heated arguments for them to get to that point; but, in the end, it's made them an extremely powerful couple with a marriage bond like no other I've seen before.

Tate and Niko have been married for a while as well; however, their relationships are completely different. Nikoli is possessive, but worships the ground his wife, Sabrina, walks on. She pretty much snaps her fingers and Niko goes running. I understand his devotion though; she was his best friend for many years besides Tate and was kidnapped right under his watch. That's how they got so deep into the sex trade mess to begin with. Sabrina's father was right in the mix of it all and pulled her under with him.

Tate and Emily have been together the longest. From the bits and pieces I've gotten over time, I've learned that he saved her life from a crazy ex-boyfriend. I guess the drama with her made him embrace his Mafiya background. He was busy hiding away, not wanting anything to do with the family business.

Sounds familiar, huh? Not only do we have similar features, but we also seem to think alike on a lot of shit too. If we'd had the chance to grow up together, I have a feeling that Tate, Viktor, and I would've been inseparable.

The day carries on much in the same fashion, with more people piling into the kitchen to find out what's going on. I end up repeating myself about what went down at least three times, and eventually we decide that it may be best if I go to the upcoming auction alone before introducing one of my cousins back into the fold.

Only I won't be completely by myself. At the next event, I'll have one or possibly a few men with me that will be posing as my guards that work for my father and me. In a sense, they really will be working for me, but when it comes down to it, their loyalty is always to Viktor.

Until then, we wait and prepare. But inside, I know that there's no possible way to make it so that my heart doesn't hurt for each and every woman I see this weekend. There's nothing that can take the innate need I have implanted in my soul to protect the weak and conquer the mighty. It may take a little time to free them; but eventually, I'll make it happen.

Some may think it's the police officer in me coming out, but being around my family, I know it's the Mafiya blood screaming in my veins. It's not a 'do-gooder' sense. It's the fact that I'm meant to be heading up a Russian empire right now. My body knows it, and it's ready for me to take control, to rule what's rightfully mine from my father.

I'm not meant to get along with the other families — the Sicilians, Cartel, Romanians — none of them. I thought I was destined to serve and protect, but for once in my life, my heritage is beating down on me. It's written in the past that I'm meant to be a King, and the scary thing is, I could do more — help more women — if I were to embrace the criminal side.

I guess the real question is, will I succumb? Only time will tell.

If you want to change the world,

go home and love your family.

-Mother Theresa

This week has spun by in a complete whirl. The chief called to update me on the Johnson case. That brought me back down to earth and got me refocused on my personal life real quickly. Nothing like hearing from the Chief of Police reassuring you that they're working to get your suspension resolved as quickly as possible so you can go back to your regular job.

I've been so wrapped up in everything with my cousins that my other life started to disappear into the background. It looks like it may stay there for a short while too. The DA is ready to close the case, but Internal Affairs is busy trying to cross their t's and dot their i's before calling it quits. It's normal. It's happened to me before, so I'm not wigging out about it. If I'm honest with myself, all I want to do at the moment is get those women free anyhow.

Johnson was a fucking slime bucket too. I'm all for the justice system. I do my best to believe in it, but he would've easily been out in five years for the penial shit the DA had on him. We all know Johnson should've been put on trial to be put away for life without parole. Death was an easy out for him, and in return, he's no longer on the streets hurting innocent people. If anything, they should be patting me on the back for what happened, not trying to find some way to scold me for it.

Am I sorry that I'm the one who shot him? Of course, everyone has a mother, brother, sister, or child out there — someone who cares for them. However, I'm not sorry that he's off the streets and can do no more harm to anyone else.

That's where Internal Affairs is giving me shit. They keep bringing up the question if it was 'just' of me to shoot to kill. What they don't get, is that being undercover with the types of criminals I'm around, you don't have time to think like that. You do your best, and sometimes you have to pick the lesser of two evils. In this case, it was kill or be killed, and I'll be damned if I was going to be gunned down by that shit stain. No one knows that feeling or how fast anything can happen. It only takes a second for a confrontation to go south.

All I can do now is hope that they come to the right decision and let me return without a slap on the wrist for anything. Bax wants to put me undercover with the Cartel when I go back. I'm thinking with this new information about the Sicilians; I may be able to dig deeper being involved with the Cartel. I'd love to be able to shut down both organizations.

I can't stand the fuckers and their shady-as-shit dealings in women and drugs. Human trafficking is my limit.

I've been thinking long and hard about this next event. I'm grateful to Viktor for letting me take some of his men with me, but there's only one person I trust to have my back besides my cousins and who's not a cop — my best friend, Finn O'Kassidy, and I need him with me.

I've met some unsavory characters in my line of work, but Finn wasn't one of them. I was undercover on a weapons bust, and my cover was damn near blown the first time we crossed paths. Finn stepped in and vouched for me. It turns out he headed up a chunk of the Irish Mob and knew I was a cop. He could've killed me and told me as much, but he didn't. His reasoning behind his free pass was that I looked just like a Russian that once did his father a favor. It turns out my father had a few friends. They're in low places, but this one paid off. Weird how you can run into someone and find out your families are intertwined in a way — one Russian, one Irish.

In return, I busted the Romanians he was trading with and left the trail to him cold. Hence, how I totaled that Mercedes Trey was giving me shit over. The chief and mayor were happy we had a big bust to make the headlines, and I had a new contact in the game. Like I said before, sometimes you have to pick the lesser of two evils. Finn's not the best person in the world, but he's not the worst criminal either, and we've become really good friends over the years.

Pulling my cell free, I dial the latest number he's given me for his burner.

"Yep?" A deep voice with a hint of Irish accent answers immediately.

"Finn."

"Dia duit."

"To you too."

"How're you doin'?"

"Could be better, but can't really complain. You?"

"A bit wrecked, drank my fair share of Guinness last night." He chuckles even though he sounds like death.

"Must be nice. I could use a night of drinking with the shit I've been dealing with."

"Come on, then."

Snickering, I shake my head as if he can see me. "If only it were that easy. I have to keep my wits about me right now. I could use a friend this weekend though."

"Oh yeah? What kind of shite have you dug up?"

"I can send the jet for you, and we can talk about it? Not the type of thing to discuss over the phone."

"Sure thing, I'm in Boston at the moment."

"Okay, I'll text you when and where."

He hangs up, and I immediately organize everything to get him here as soon as possible. Tomorrow's already Friday, and I'll be headed to New York. I have less than twenty-four hours to get Finn on board with me and ready.

I'm not worried, though. I know once he finds out what's happening, he'll want in. He deals in weapons like my cousins, and if he so much as wished a poor thought on a woman, his mother would lynch him. I've met her, sweet woman, but a heart of steel when it comes to 'her boys' as she calls the thugs that Finn's in charge of. She demands them to show all women respect and a 'soft hand' — her words.

Another thing that's been on my mind and in my dreams when I finally make myself close my eyes is Sasha. She held far too much of my attention the last time I was around her, and I'm worried she'll do the same tomorrow night. I'm not looking forward to the possible shit storm tomorrow at all, but I am counting down the minutes it seems until I get to be with her again. I don't know why she's any different than the others, but she stuck out to me.

Watching her close to Yema and the way he treated her made my skin crawl. I wanted just to snatch her away from him and tell him to fuck off. But...I couldn't. I had to hold back and play their sick, stupid game. The more I have to go to these events, the more chances I'll get to memorize the faces of the men there buying up the women. I'll get to them eventually, and if I don't, I'll be sure to fill Viktor in about each one of them.

"Ready for tomorrow?"

I turn to Tate as he comes to stand next to me. I've been out back of Viktor's cabin, making calls. "No, but I will be by the time I hit New York. I don't have another choice."

"Anything I can do?"

"Thanks, but no. I have Finn coming in. I'm going to talk him into going with me. I can't ask Morelli for anything else right now. Bad enough I had to say we'd owe him a favor. I was expecting you to go along with it and Viktor to be pretty pissed over it. He surprised me by taking it so well. "

"He knows you'd never do it unless you felt you had to. I don't know why it still shocks me that you're close friends with the leader of the Irish mob. Oh, yeah I do, probably because you're from a Russian crime family and you're also a cop. You realize you contradict basically every stereotype people have about us?"

"And you're close friends with a ruthless group of bikers. Maybe it's a family trait?"

"You have a point." He nods, snickering. "Anyhow, they sent me out here to let you know that dinner's about to be ready. I'll let Vik know that Finn's coming. I'm assuming it'll be tonight?"

"Yeah, I just texted Victor to ask for the jet. I'm hoping it can pick up Finn as soon as possible."

"If not, you're welcome to ours. Neither of us is going anywhere tonight."

"I appreciate it. I may take you up on it going to New York if you don't mind?"

"Of course not; consider it done." He nods, going back inside.

Five years since I started coming around and the Mafiya's aged him. I don't know how he puts up with some of the stuff they deal with. I think if it weren't for Emily, he'd completely lose it. It's what I'm afraid of myself as I go down this rabbit hole, toward who knows what.

"Well, there's the bastard that sent me on a late night flight!" Finn booms as he descends the private plane's stairs.

It's four a.m. so I get why he may not be too excited. I've had three hours of sleep, and I feel like I've been run over. We were going over the game plan all last night.

"I brought coffee," I grumble.

"Aye, but did you bring whiskey with it?"

"I'm sure you had plenty on your flight." He pulls me in for a man hug. Once we became friends, he told me that he's a hugger. He said too many people that come into his life don't get to stick around long enough. They leave bloody and early, so he'd rather hug you in case he never sees you again.

"You bet your sweet little cop arse I did. It's the least you Russians can do." He winks, and I hand over the steaming cup of Joe. He takes a sip as we head toward the waiting SUV. "Now that's some good shite. Put some hair on yer chest."

"Viktor's wife makes it. She gets it flown in from Columbia."

"Ye fuckers are weird; ya know that? I've never met a bunch of mobsters who's friends with people in strange places."

"Oh, she doesn't know anyone over there; she gets it off Amazon I think."

He nods, climbing in the passenger seat and I round to the driver's side.

"Nice wheels, you steal it?"

"Why would I steal it? I'm a cop, remember?"

"That I do, but you've been with your kin. Figured they'd be teaching you the proper way to be a criminal."

I chuckle again. He's always saying crazy shit. He no doubt drank his weight in liquor on the way over if he's this wound up.

"We're getting back on a plane in a few hours, so you should try to sleep."

"The fuck we are?"

"Yep, we're going to New York."

"For shite's sake, you shoulda picked me up on the way then."

"I didn't think of it. Besides, we have a lot to cover. Tonight's going to be interesting…that's for sure."

Sapphire Knight

Damaged people are dangerous

because they know they can

survive.

-LoveFromASelfHarmer

Sasha

I hate this man standing beside The Master. I hate him so much; I wish he would choke on his own spit and die. The things Yema does to us—to me—are sickening. I thought the man from last weekend was going to take me away, but Yema wouldn't allow it. I swear he only did it so he could get another week to degrade me further.

"Girl!" It's said with distaste by the Master, as if I'm the scum on the bottom of their shoes.

I never understood why they put us through all of this if they hate us so much. Why keep us prisoner? Why keep us locked up away from other people? You'd think if we were such a burden they'd kick us to the street. I often wish they would. I'd much rather sleep on a dirty street curb than here on a clean sheet only to be roused whenever one of them is bored or looking to get off.

"He said, 'Girl'!" The mean one yells again. This time a bookend flies toward my head. It crashes against the wall beside me, and I swear fury fills Yema's eyes at the loud thump it makes hitting the drywall.

"Yes, Master? How can I serve you?" I go to him, getting to my knees in front of him, pretending to worship him, as he wishes us to do. He thinks he's the creator of all things, the one to offer us life, the Master. I've blocked out most of my feelings toward him, but I can't help the craving in the pit of my stomach. I want to bend over and bite his ankle. Make him fall over, clutching the limb in pain. I want him to feel just an ounce of what the guard's grip is like on the new women—the bite of pain from their strong fingers and hands as they control you.

He's wrong about being the one to save and provide for us. I remember my mother, the one who filled my heart with warmth and safety. I never had to fear her when she raised her hand or called my name.

My name...I can't even remember my real name anymore. Was it Sasha? Or did they just pick a new Russian name and make me believe it belonged to me all along?

"I don't see why anyone would want you with how slow you are." He scowls, his cold, beady eyes glaring down at me. I could say the same about him, but I don't. He would hurt me if I did; I've learned to remain silent.

It drives me crazy, but even full of bitterness, his features are handsome. Maybe because I don't ever remember having a father and this man has given me what little I do have? The others here I hate more, like Yema. They touch and hurt me whenever the Master gives them permission. It's been so long now; I don't even get sick from it anymore. I just make it fade away.

I remain quiet as I'm supposed to. I'm not allowed to speak. Sometimes I'll mess up, but I try not to. His hand comes hard and fast when I don't mind his rules. His rules are everything here; it's how you stay alive. Learn the rules, live them, and survive.

Is it the businessman from the event who's interested in me, I wonder? Could he be talking about the tattooed man who looked at Yema like he wanted to cut his throat from one side to the other? The handsome one, who stared at me like he was hungry for me?

I hope so. He wasn't friendly, but he had kind eyes. I've met very few men with a kindness shining in them like he had. Here you learn very quickly which men are the bad ones by the way they look at you.

"You need to be ready for tonight. Go to the room and prepare yourself. Do not make Yema wait for you." He flicks his hand off to the side as if to shoo me away.

"Yes, Master," I reply, staring at his feet until he's turned away and my gaze is met with the white fur from the rug I'm kneeling on. Only once he's turned his back on me, do I stand and make my way to the basement. I would love to drive a knife through him from this angle, but I'd never make it. They always leave us weak, so we don't have the strength to fight back.

Yema promised Mr. Masterson that he could take me this weekend. I've prayed every morning and every night that *he* remembers, that *he* comes back for *me*. He took Trixie, the angel haired one, last weekend. But that's okay. I'll be his new favorite, I know it; and if not, I'll kill her.

"Ready?" I glance down at the fresh suit my cousin gave me to wear. He said I couldn't show up in the same as last week. I don't give a shit, though. I'm not wasting money on clothes that I won't wear again after this is all over with. This was the compromise. I didn't have to spend any money, and Viktor got his way as well with me wearing a new suit.

"I'm pretty sure these fuckers will shoot me, and I'm not on their magical list. They don't like the Irish."

"You're my guest that I'm bringing and you have money. I don't think they'll mind you spending it at their event. They won't if they have an ounce of common sense."

"Aye, you owe me somethin' good for this one, lad."

"I owe you? Nope, this is what it's like having friends. You do shit for each other."

"I don't come through California asking you to transport shipments for me."

"That's different; I'm a cop."

"Yet yer asking me to buy women. Not seeing much difference in our levels of criminal deeds. Except yours is with humans and mine is with metal objects."

I huff. I'm not buying the women to satisfy my sexual needs, but to save them. Big difference compared to shipping and distributing illegal weapons to more criminals out in the streets. I'd understand if I were buying the women to resell them or for my sexual pleasure.

Finn straightens his own black suit as we pull up to the museum, and I hand my rental keys over to the eager valet standing out front. There are twenty or so young guys in burgundy and black jackets running around, parking everyone's vehicles and escorting them up the grand staircase.

"Name sir?" an expensively dressed man at the door asks, with slicked back hair, peering down at a tablet.

"Beau Masterson and guest." I can't believe I have to use that last name. I wonder if I'll ever get used to it. I have to think of it as an undercover assignment—different clothes, name and city to do a job, like usual. At least it's not my father's last name and only my cousins'. Going with my first name keeps it simpler, and if anyone digs far enough, they'll see my father does indeed have a son named Beau. Thankfully, Masters isn't linked to my birth certificate they'd find, or else they'd also discover what I do for a living.

"There's no 'with guest' listed on my list, Mr. Masterson," the stuffy doorman answers. He glances at Finn from head to toe and then back up again, meeting his annoyed stare. "Your name, sir?"

"Finn O'Kassidy, the Irish stallion," he throws in, and I snort to myself. Cocky fucker.

"Nope, you're not on the list."

With a huff, I butt in. "Yema Capelloni invited me, and I'm bringing a guest with me. Now tell your boss to fix it. He'll want to see me, and now he'll want to see Finn here, as well."

The guy places his hand on his ear, talking into his wrist like he's fucking 007 or some shit. He nods a few times while looking me over with curious glances.

"Excuse me for that misunderstanding, just doing my job," he finally says. "Mr. Capelloni welcomes you both and hopes you will have an enjoyable evening."

"Well then, that's the spirit, lad!" Finn smacks the guy on the shoulder and struts right on by.

I follow with a sharp nod in door guy's direction. "Plan on it." Mumbling, I snatch the first glass of bubbly wine off a passing server's tray. It tastes disgusting like sour grapes and fizz, so I quickly discard it on a table. "Be nice to get a beer."

Finn overhears me and perks up, "Now yer talkin' or maybe some whiskey?"

"Careful with the liquor tonight, remember what I told you happened to me last weekend." He nods, his eyes smiling, thinking I'm a weak drinker. I'm serious, though; I know I was drugged with something. I'll find out soon enough once I piss hot.

"Gentlemen, welcome!" Yema greets in his heavy accent, approaching us with a smug smirk planted on his face. Finn's nose scrunches up like he's had a whiff of some bad fish but shakes the hand offered his way.

"Yema Capelloni, meet Finn O'Kassidy." With him by my side, I was able to get away with leaving the few guards at the plane instead of bringing them with us. They're here in the city if I sense trouble and need some backup; otherwise, they're out of my way so we can keep a low profile about us. Finn is merciless when it comes to surviving. I have no doubt if we were in a beat down of some sort or trading fire, he could easily hold his own beside me.

"Mr. Masterson." Yema offers his hand after exchanging fake pleasantries with Finn. The name grates on my nerves and I feel like scraping a knife down the center of his face. "I assure you, everything is in place for this evening. I'm confident you'll be highly pleased with our offerings."

"Good to hear."

I want to ask where Sasha is but hold myself back, not wanting to come off as too eager. I only need a glimpse just to make sure she's here tonight. I've thought of her all week, and there's no way she can be as beautiful as I remember. I think I've built her up in my mind over the days.

Speaking of beautiful, Willow is already starting to bloom in our care. She's been eating good meals all week. She can't have a lot of food or else she'll get sick from being starved for so long, but just the infusion of vitamins in her system is making a huge difference. Viktor had a doctor come over the day after she arrived and injected her with a few vitamin shots and a saline drip so she'd be hydrated as well. We plan to do the same for all of the other women too.

She's been so gracious about anything and everything offered to her and Alexei has taken her under his wing like a weak kitten. I'm pretty sure he's smitten with her already.

She does, however, have nightmares. They're bad. Alexei says he wakes her up two, sometimes three, times a night. Whatever these fuckheads did to her in the past was in no way pleasant with the dreams that plague her so gravely each time she closes her eyes in the dark.

We showed up kind of late tonight, but it was done on purpose. I'm not here to support the charity. As fucked up as that may seem, it's the truth. I'm here for two things: Sasha and however many other women I can get out safely without raising suspicion.

My father's capped me at nine hundred thousand from his account and Viktor has offered me an additional five hundred thousand. I don't know if it'll get me many women, or if any at all to be honest. I told them that, but they reminded me that we don't want to put too much money into their auctions or the puppets making them happen will become even more powerful.

I understand their opinions, and I agree with them, but if someone outbids me for Sasha I may end up murdering them, and that's not like me. There's something about seeing her frail body that has made me want to protect her like no other. Of course, it's a woman to bring this side out of me; look at my cousins and how they act with their spouses. They'd slay a thousand men for their wives if needed.

I remember the first time that I met their women—they're twin sisters, so it's even crazier. I'd asked them if they had a triplet for me. I thought it was hilarious, but they didn't quite agree. I guess they found out about each other by mistake, and when I asked about another sister, they were a little leery of responding.

A middle-aged woman in an emerald-colored ball gown takes off with Finn, pulling him onto the dance floor and I can't help but think it's funny. Leave it to the lady in green to pick out the full-blooded Irishman in the room.

The night dwindles on, much in the same fashion as Chicago, and I find myself wasting away the time by eating too many almonds and drinking a few beers. This place has a small bar, and I made sure the bartender handed me the beer bottles so I could open them myself. I'm not about to let anyone slip something into my drinks again. I can't believe I fell for that rookie mistake last weekend.

"Mr. Masterson." The older guy that tried to speak with me last week approaches. He gave me his card, but later on, when I went to dig it out, it was gone. I don't know how I could've lost it unless it somehow fell out when I was sleeping on the plane ride home.

"Excuse me, but I am at a loss for your name. I don't know what happened to your card."

He holds out his hand, and I shake it, my grip slightly too tight. I want anyone and everyone here intimidated by me as much as possible. It'll help keep me alive.

"I understand." He digs in his inside jacket pocket and hands me a new one.

"Thank you, Mr…" Glancing at the cardstock, it's only a phone number, no name. I place this one in my inside suit pocket. I'll do a search later and see if I can find any information on him.

110

"You may call me Tory. I see you've been keeping busy with the finger foods."

"Yeah, they obviously don't believe in chicken wings or anything good."

He chuckles. He doesn't seem so bad, to be honest, but nonetheless, he's a criminal, and I'll figure out who he really is, soon enough.

"I could go for those little slider burgers you get during football season."

"Those are good too."

"So, I was hoping to speak with you this past week. I wanted to introduce myself last weekend. I was friends with Victor once upon a time."

"I see. He's no longer in charge." The other Viktor, my cousin who was named after Victor, my father, has taken his place.

His smile has a touch of sadness to it. "I know. I was sorry to see him go, but alas I understand. We must all retire at some point, I suppose."

"Do you really understand? You know how he was dragging our family through the mud with his distasteful habits?" Keeping my voice neutral is tough. Knowing what my father had his hands in is like painting me red, being related to him.

"I'm afraid I do. It may not make a difference to you, but he thought he was helping people."

I keep my voice down, partially wondering if this is a test. "By dealing in human trafficking and prostitution? Oh, and let's not forget all of the narcotics as well."

"Many of those women were drug addicts when he found them. They got clean under his care. Yes, he sold them, but they never went to bad men. They went to influential men who didn't have time for a wife but wanted someone to be there when they could make it home."

"Sounds like they should've gotten a cat."

"In a sense, yes. I guess in a way, that's what they were paying your father for. They'd get a willing woman who needed to be taken care of financially. The women would get security and a sort of stability. I understand why you may not care for your father, but he wasn't completely corrupt in his ministrations."

So he does know who I am. I don't know if I should just be surprised or a bit worried; there's no telling who else knows who I am if he was able to figure it out.

"Well, we'll just have to agree to disagree."

He nods. "Isn't that why you're here; to offer them a better life than what they obviously have?"

I find myself being a little too honest with him. "Am I that easy to read?"

"No. I just know who your family is. Gizya's boys have done a decent job of cleaning up their business, but in doing

112

so, they don't see everything going on behind the scenes anymore."

"But you knew who my father was without me telling you."

"Indeed I did. Perhaps I've known you a lot longer than you suspect, and it was like coming across a face from the past when you came down to that basement."

His words take me off guard. Do I know this man? And how? Who is he really?

We're interrupted by another hostess announcing that the evening's events are over. We all know it's a front though, a ploy to introduce the real festivities that the men all came here for.

Finn kisses the green dress woman's cheek and comes to stand at my side. "Are we leaving? I thought we were here for more?" he questions, and when I look over to Tory, he's already walked off toward the elevators. I have about a million things I want to ask him now, but it'll have to wait.

"No, we're staying. This is what happened last time too." His eyes light up, remembering everything I told him from earlier. I wasn't too specific how it went down; I was mostly vocal about what went on at the auction. "The guy that was just over here was the one I mentioned to you who tried to speak to me last time."

"What did he want tonight?"

"To introduce himself and basically tell me that my father isn't so bad."

He snorts and rolls his eyes, mimicking my thoughts exactly. Leave it to a fellow criminal to justify another's reasoning and actions.

"Right," I agree. "I'm hitting the bathroom then we can head downstairs. I can't believe that idiot didn't let me see Sasha yet."

"Shady fucker no doubt. You think he's up to somethin'?"

"I don't know. I didn't see any of the women out and about at the charity last week either. They were kept away from it, and then shown off once we all got down to the basement."

"Then get the ruffles from yer arse and let's go take care of some business."

I have been fighting since I was

a child. I am not a survivor,

I am a warrior.

-The Success Club

Sasha

"I've changed my mind," Yema mutters, his lips downturned in disgust. "I'm making the stupid Russian wait another week. He'll pay more if he thinks there's something special about you."

"No, please?" The plea leaves my lips before I have a chance to taper it away. I know better than to show them something I want. It's best to make them believe everything about you is gone that you wish for nothing. They discover one little thing, and they use it to control you.

His evil-sounding laugh rings out, drawing the attention of the other women waiting to be thrown onto the stage and sold to the first wealthy pig who's willing to spend some money. "What is this, girl? You think this is some fairy tale?"

"No...I..."

"Have you forgotten your visit from Boris? He is Russian, the same as Masterson. They won't give you pleasure. They'll fuck you and kill you, that is how all Russians are."

It's on the tip of my tongue to argue. Beau's nothing like Boris. I don't know him well, but I do know what I saw when looking at him. He is Russian, yes, but not all men from my beloved country are like Yema says.

I remember being a little girl and seeing the baker nearly every week. He'd offer me treats each time my mother would take me with her. If he were evil, as Yema claims, he'd have never cared about showing kindness to a young girl. Those were some of the best memories I have.

I miss my mom, but I was separated from her at such a young age that sometimes my memories of her begin to feel as if they're fading. I remember the night everything changed like it was yesterday, though. We were walking home, and it was evening time.

The air was chilly because I was in a bright red pea coat. It was my absolute favorite. The fabric made from wool was so warm, and it had big black buttons down the front.

I was holding her soft hand, swinging them between us as I skipped along beside her. Her hands were always there, embracing me in some way. I loved the affection that she so openly showed me. I was humming a song, and she kept singing little bits of words to it; she only knew a few here and there. Her voice was beautiful. She always sang the prettiest at Christmas time when we had carols to keep busy with.

I ran the song through my mind, giggling each time she had to make up a word because she'd forgotten the correct one. I felt her hand give me a quick tug, and when I glanced back, her eyes were wide. She was scared, and I quickly turned back to look in front of me, but there was nothing.

I peered her way again, and there was a big man standing directly behind her. He had long, dark hair, shadowing part of his face full of overgrown wiry hair. His hand was wrapped around her neck as he tried to drag her backward. She fought; I know she did with all her might. But my mother was a delicate woman, always giving me any extra food we may have had, so I was never hungry. I didn't realize it then, but she was starving herself. I know now that's most likely the real reason the baker gave me treats on each visit. He always stared at Mother with kind, worried eyes.

Mother's grip on my hand was tight. It increased until I called out, yelling for the mean man to let her go. I was fierce at one time—not this meek shell of a human being I've become.

I yelled, sternly, "You let my mother go!" Only he didn't listen. His hand grew tighter like a vice until my sweet mother's face was red and puffy, as she gasped for air and clawed at his arm with her free hand.

Eventually, she had to let go of me to fight against him harder, only it was no use. She was no match for the overgrown brute. He started dragging her toward a dark corner, and I charged. So brave for a tiny girl, I was determined to save her like one of the superheroes I'd seen on our sorry excuse of a television. The picture was so bad, and the cartoons came across as fuzzy. It didn't matter, though; none of that stuff did. I didn't care she had to find our furniture next to dumpsters or make potatoes for dinner a few nights a week. I was proud of her—I loved her.

Wearing a fierce expression with a fiery growl, I lunged and was stopped by a strong grasp on my shoulder. Stunned, I glanced up into a much younger Master's eyes. I think my heart faltered a bit gazing up at such a powerful man. I had nothing on him, and I knew it. Still, not one to give up, I pushed and pulled against him, kicking out and swiping my nails at his face the same way I'd gotten in trouble at school for doing. It was like swatting at a fly. He chuckled, his eyes full of amusement as he ducked and weaved to miss my hits.

I fought the hardest that day like nothing was going to stop me. I was determined to help my mother—to rescue her. The Master's steel-like arms wrapped around me securely, until I could barely squirm and I was a good squirmer; my mother told me so, many times when she'd wrap me up in my favorite blanket.

I stared off in the direction I'd last seen her sea blue eyes, wide and frightened. She was gone at that moment like she'd never existed, and my life was changed forever. As the Master loaded me up in his big, fancy car, I could've sworn I heard her scream.

Yema picks up a lacy bra, flinging it at me.

"Undress. You'll wear this. Maybe the others will bid on you, and he'll spend more on you in the end. You better make money, or you'll go back."

Obeying immediately, I shuck out of the plain, white nightgown. It's what they make us wear when we're not at one of these events. The Master says it's cheap and offers them an easy view if they want it. I don't want to upset Yema in any way; I want to go away from this place with my gentlemen. I want him to keep me.

Yema's calculating gaze watches me closely as I stand naked in front of him, struggling a few seconds until I get the bra clasp hooked behind me, securing it around my small breasts. There's nothing extraordinary about them, but I hope they will please Mr. Masterson in some way.

Hearing his last name at first made me falter with unease. Going from the man I've called Master for so long to someone who's last name is quite close, frightens me a bit.

I watched him as much as I could get away with in Chicago and he surprised me. He didn't kiss Yema's feet as so

119

many of the others do; but instead, he stared at him with a stern, angry gaze. It pleased me beyond words with how ugly Yema can be to me and the other women he brings to sell.

There have been many nights I've thought of killing Yema and the Master. I'd never do it though; I'd never succeed. They're too strong, and I'm always afraid I'll die doing it. I never have the energy either. How can a tiny person like myself hope to kill a man when I never know if I'll randomly pass out.

"Now the skirt." Yema throws a shred of material at me.

It hits my face, a piece of the fabric going in my eye. It stings enough that they try to tear up, but it's hard to cry when you don't have a lot of extra fluids in your body. I stopped crying over things long ago. Now I just exist through them.

I step into the skirt and slide the short stretchy fabric over my legs. It's loose around my waist, but the spandex in the material will help keep it in place for as long as I'm on stage. I wish he would've given me some panties to wear with it, but of course, he pushes those off to the side. While I want to hide as much of myself from the old vultures fluttering about the room out there, Yema and the Master want me to flaunt too much.

I've seen the men at these events many times. They either like the women quiet and meek or readily showing off their goods. There's no middle, it seems. The Master claims

120

that I'm lucky to get to come to these places with Yema, that I have a better chance than all the other women.

I don't see it, though. If anything, it makes me more frightened because I know once most of these men are finished doing their business with their purchases, that the ladies will be killed. I'm miserable in life, but I don't wish to die.

He claims this is a privilege that I had to earn the opportunity to be seen on Yema's arm. Personally, the man makes me sick, and every weekend I pray one of these men will stab him to death and I'll escape. The chances of someone killing him are decent; as for my escape though, not so much.

And then there was my gentleman. Could I really have gotten so fortunate to meet a man who would want me and not kill me afterward? Was the Master right all along about me having a better chance than the others? I've been to ten of these events and last week was the first time a man specifically asked for me. Of course, they'd made suggestions in the past, but Yema always shot it down, claiming I was no good. Was this man someone special that he's changed his mind? Was he different than all the others? Who is he?

"Come on; you're going out there first. Those imbeciles are always overeager to bid and go home early. It's the late buyers who have less money."

Following behind Yema, I remain silent, my stomach twirling at a ridiculous speed making me nauseous. What if he doesn't like me? What if he's not pleased once he sees me naked? What if someone else buys me?

"Don't look so…whatever it is that's wrong with your face."

God forbid I be sad or nervous. Of course, I'm happy to be away from him and the other evil men they bring around, but there's still fear of the unknown. I flash a fake grin that I'm sure resembles a grimace.

"You don't make money, you'll go back, and you won't like it, girl."

He calls everyone girl. I wish he'd trip and face plant right now.

Victoria, the Master's niece announces my name. "Here's sexy Sasha! Get your money ready, gentlemen."

These are not gentlemen. These are men with mean eyes just like the Master's. I take one step onto the large, black stage. This stage doesn't have the catwalk feel like the last. The stage here is flat against the far wall, maybe six feet wide, twenty feet long and five feet off the ground. I'm supposed to walk the entire length so all the men standing in front of it can see me.

Taking one step in front of the other, the dim lighting illuminating over the crowd helps me block out their faces a bit. The overhead lights above me are strikingly bright, and there's so many that I instantly feel warmer walking underneath them. I put another foot in front, and the first degrading remark hits my skin like a whip. Then another slams into me, burning my flesh and hurting my soul. I pass one man after another, their comments becoming cruder as I go, and I find myself seeking one face in particular as my body shakes, plagued with nerves.

Beau.

Once I pick his handsome features out of the crowd, I train my gaze directly on him, ignoring everyone else in the room. One step, then another… I'm nearly to him when my head suddenly becomes dizzy. My fingers feel like they have tingles in them and then everything goes black.

The men mulling around the poorly-lit lower level room have my stomach turning. The low-ball tumblers of dark liquid being handed out by the few servers look more enticing with each passing moment. That refreshing drink could assist in dulling the senses and help everything appear a bit less twisted than it is.

Finn sighs, his eyes a bit weary as he glances around.

"See?"

He nods. "I do. I've been ta one before, unfortunately."

His response takes me off guard; I had no idea. He's never mentioned anything about it in the past, but I guess he wouldn't have. He should've let me know something on the plane.

"When?"

He shrugs. "I was a young lad. Never went back after that. There's something creepy about it all. Too many women want a bad boy anyhow, no need ta waste this sort of money when you can find a willing one."

The intercom comes on, welcoming us all to the night's 'most anticipated event.' The losers all crowd around the stage, but we stay back waiting until it's time for us. These guys up front will all bid on the first thing that walks out, just like last weekend, but I'm waiting for one woman in particular, along with a special group they're supposed to have picked out for me. No doubt they'll try auctioning them off in front of me, to get more money. Bastards. They're stupid if they don't realize that I know that much of their plan.

"Sasha! Get your money ready, gentlemen." I catch the ending, but it was enough for me to make out her name.

Fuck.

"Come on," I grunt and elbow my way through to the front. This wasn't supposed to go down like this. I'm guessing that assface, Yema, is doing this shit on purpose to throw me off.

I'm at the end of the stage, but at least I have a good spot to bid on her and hear the others if they bid as well. If…who am I kidding? Of course, they'll bid on her. She may have been bruised up and skinny last weekend, but there's fire underneath it all.

Sasha walks on stage, stiff as a board. Her footsteps appear heavy as her strides are so small like she's dreading the walk, and who can blame her. As she approaches, her face grows ashier with each step. I wish I knew the thoughts running through her mind to have that look resting on her face. She's still beautiful, but that can't distract me. Not tonight and not ever. I have to help her, not consume her like my own thoughts have insisted I do—taunting me with the memory of her beauty all week.

She gets nearer to our spot, and as she approaches, I can hear the lewd comments from every asshole she passes. Their taunting words ignite a rage inside me, and I have to hold my breath to keep from pummeling a few of them. I'm not here for them, at least not yet. If I get the chance to put a few behind bars, it'll be icing on the cake.

Sasha's willowy body wavers a bit as she takes another step, her gaze finally landing on me. I think it brings her a sense of peace as hope enlightens her irises just a smidge. Her foot lifts for another step, and I can't help but silently cheer her on. *Come on, baby, you can do this, almost to me.*

And then her eyes roll back, her body falling to the floor in a heap, out cold.

I'm the first one on the stage, my training kicking in. My fingertips go to her neck, checking for her pulse. Closing my eyes, I concentrate on the beats, counting. Her pulse is there; it's not quite at a resting rate which isn't good. It should be at least slightly elevated with what was just going on.

She's not as healthy as she needs to be, that's for sure. It angers me and makes my stomach sick inside at the same time. I hate these people, and I've never wanted to kill these assholes more than I do right now.

It worries me, but she should be okay. I'm guessing it's my prior diagnosis of the women being dehydrated and malnourished. The event tonight probably pushed her over, burning through what little she had saved up inside that was keeping her going.

Yema strolls over casually, appearing bored. Victoria, the announcer, remains at her podium, eyes sad, while the other men in the room use this as a bathroom and refill break.

"I knew she was weak." Yema shrugs. "We'll dispose of her and find you a replacement."

The growl that leaves my throat is so deep and feral you'd swear it was from an animal and not a man. Gruffly, I scowl, "You won't touch her. I told you I wanted her."

"They usually die fairly quickly once they start passing out like this. Unless you like them unresponsive?" He asks this like it's a normal request and fuck if I don't want to upchuck at the thought.

126

"How much?" grates out between a few breaths as I rein my temper in. This guy will get it, maybe not right this moment, but at some point, it'll happen.

He shrugs, sighing in exasperation. "I don't care, five hundred thousand? She's pretty useless to me at this point."

"Fifty thousand and I take her now."

"I can get that when she's dead...one hundred thousand."

"Done. Bill me and have the other group for me next weekend. I'm not waiting around when she needs an IV. And make sure the group I buy don't fucking pass out. Try feeding them."

His eyebrow cocks and Finn steps beside me, arms crossed over his chest, staring Yema down crossly.

"As you wish, Mr. Masterson." His mask shutters over his face again as he takes a step back and mock bows.

I'm going to teach this pissant some manners. Standing, I hike Sasha over my shoulder. I need to get her to the private plane ASAP.

Sapphire Knight

Strong women still need

their hands held.

-Truth

Sasha

For once in a very long time, my body feels warm all over, and I don't have the constant ache in my stomach from never eating as much as I'd like to. Opening my eyes, I find a light blanket tucked all around me. I feel funny, like I'm in a vehicle, only I'm laid out on a bed. It's comfortable with a black and grey duvet covering it. There are probably ten pillows surrounding me as well.

Where am I?

I start to sit up when something stings my arm. I start to jerk it when a gruff voice halts me.

"Careful, there's a needle in your arm. I don't want you to yank it out or hurt yourself." My eyes find the owner of the voice. It's my Mr. Masterson.

My gaze flies to my arm, where indeed there's a needle taped securely in the crook. A tiny tube pushes clear liquid into me.

He's drugging me? But he doesn't have to. I want to be here with him. I've seen what's happened to the other girls when they put stuff into their arms. They end up going crazy from it. I don't want that for me. I can serve him without it.

"I-I..." I clear my throat, dry from sleep and try again. "Please," I plead. I know not to speak unless he asks it of me; I know not to go against his wishes. I grew up learning these things from the Master.

"Please, what?" he asks, my eyes growing wide that he's actually asking me what I want to say. It's never mattered in the past.

"Please stop the drugs. I will obey without them, I promise."

Scowling, he stands and paces in front of the bed, like a caged animal, ready to break free. "That's an IV with saline. I'm not drugging you; I'm making you better."

A tear trails over my cheek. I have no idea what he means.

"What now?"

"I'm not good enough. I'm sorry, I will be better."

"No." He shakes his head. "You don't know what saline is?"

"I don't, I apologize."

"Stop apologizing. You were dehydrated and passed out. You fell to the floor. You needed fluids in your body to get well again; that's what this clear stuff is doing. It's making your body heal. As will the vitamin shots you received. The B12 should give you some energy. I'm sure you have a deficiency of everything at this point. But we'll get all of that fixed with food and whatever the doctor suggests when we land."

I don't know what he means with vitamins and stuff. Master never gave me any of that sort. He said I needed water and enough food to live, that's all. The shots would explain why my thigh feels so heavy though. I push the covers aside to look at the area, noticing I'm in an oversized white t-shirt.

Does he dress us like the Master also?

My leg is covered in a massive bruise, and as much as I'm used to pain, I still wince looking at it.

"You fell on that side on the stage. Can I get you to drink—a protein shake?"

"Yes, anything you'd like." I nod, keeping my features neutral. I've had protein bars before, and I enjoyed them. I hope this is the same thing. He pokes his head out the door for a minute then closes it again.

"How are you feeling?"

"I'm fine. I won't cause you any trouble, I swear. Once this clear stuff is out, I will do whatever you wish."

"Look, I'm nothing like those other guys. I won't hurt you. You can talk. Yema is nowhere close to us, and even if he were, he couldn't touch you now. Talk, ask questions, take a shower, sleep, whatever sounds good. Just take it easy, so you get well."

"I can ask you a question?"

"Of course, ask away."

"Where are we?"

"We're on my father's private plane. That's where we're going right now."

"To your father's?"

"Yes."

"Am I to be his?"

"No...listen to me Sasha, you don't belong to anyone."

Tears fill my eyes at his words. I thought I was on stage to become his? I don't want to have to go back. He's already been more kind to me in this conversation than Yema ever has over many years.

"Hey, don't cry. It's okay, I promise."

I nod, stunned inside that my body's producing tears again. Is that from the saline? There's a knock at the door, and then another guy pokes his head inside. He glances over at me, offering a lopsided grin and holds out a large glass with a straw to Mr. Masterson.

"This is my buddy, Finn. He won't hurt you either."

Finn smiles wider. "Nope, sure won't, lass. You let me know if I can help ya, 'kay?"

I nod again, shocked at how he speaks to me—how they both do. He's friendly. Only a few of the Master's men were ever semi-kind to me before.

The door closes again, and my handsome gentleman brings the glass with him.

"You probably won't be able to drink it all. It's thick, and if I know Finn, he most likely mixed this with ice cream, so you may get a sugar rush, too."

"Ice cream?" I ask, not familiar and his eyes grow sad.

"Yes, Sasha. It's good, try it."

Taking a small sip at first, I nearly want to guzzle it as the flavor explodes over my tongue. It's cold and delicious.

"What is it?" I ask after swallowing a few large mouthfuls.

"It's a chocolate protein shake. But they're usually not that great. It's Finn's doing, mixing it with ice cream that makes it so good." He smiles, and it's awe-inspiring. I've never seen a man so good-looking in my life as when he's happy and his hazel irises are sparkling.

I must gawk because he swallows hastily and pushes the glass in my direction, so I'll hold it for myself. He has me in a daze staring at him, and it's a little embarrassing. I would get punished for gaping before, but Mr. Masterson says he's not like them. Does that mean it's okay for me to look at him?

I sip another big gulp, my stomach already growing full. "Thank you, Mr. Masterson." My eyes stay trained on my lap as I say it.

His large hand, lays over my free one, lightly, drawing me back toward him. "It's nothing, and my name's Beau."

"Beau." It leaves my lips on a breath, wispy and low.

He clears his throat, standing from my side of the bed. "You finish up whatever you can drink. I'll be back to check on you."

We land, and I have her hold onto her IV drip while I carry her, princess style. She's on her second dose, so I'm hoping she'll be feeling better in no time. I checked on her once earlier, and she had been asleep again. I couldn't stop gazing at her when she appeared so peaceful. Simply put, whoever did this is a monster.

She's perfect—beyond perfect—and they were slowly killing her. How can you ruin something so trusting and pure?

Her face when she tried the shake nearly brought tears to my own eyes, and I'm not a man who cries. I'm not soft or caring for the most part, but it killed me inside knowing she'd never had something so simple as ice cream. How long did they have her? Has she ever had a normal life?

The officer in me has me wanting to interrogate her about every little detail I can get, but I'm holding myself back not wanting to overwhelm her just yet. I have to keep reminding myself that victims need time to recover and process things. I'd called my father as soon as one of Viktor's men had an IV in her arm and told him to have a doctor waiting for us. I did the basics with what we had available, but I need a professional to do a closer look.

"We're going to your home now?" she asks, her face so close to mine as I load her into the waiting town car my father sent for us. Her lips are near enough I could easily brush mine across them, but I won't. She's not here for that, and I'm a pig for even imagining it.

"No little dove, we're going to my fathers. His place is big enough for all of us, and we can keep you safe there."

"I forgot, sleeping so much."

"No worries." I climb in beside her, and she lies across the black leather seat, her head in my lap. She's completely trusting and does it automatically without hesitation. Regular people don't act like this when you first meet them. Sasha's like a sweet kitten — curling up to you and seeking whatever attention you'll shed on her. "How are you feeling?" One hand rests on the seat beside me, while I use the other to brush her hair away from her face.

Finn sits in the front, quiet beside the driver.

Her eyes flutter close, and she practically purrs with the small touch of affection I show her. I'm honestly not sure how to act with her. I've been around many victims, but this feels so much more personal to me.

She's a grown woman, but I can tell she's been morphed into whatever Yema and those around him wanted her to be. I need to tread carefully. I'm sure she already feels completely lost with all the changes, and it hasn't even been a full twenty-four hours yet.

"I feel good." Her eyes meet mine. "Better than I have in a long time."

Brushing over her forehead lightly, I send her a soft smile. "I'm glad. Keep resting so you feel even better, okay?"

She nods, her eyes closing again as she leans her cheek toward my thigh, burrowing more. She's so close and so fucking beautiful, I'm scared she's going to notice the chub resting in my pants. I can't help it. I'm torn between being angry as all fuck and turned on. I want to gut them for treating her like this. A police officer or not, this has my Mafiya genes bubbling to the top.

I roused Sasha a bit moving her from the car to the house but was able to get her tucked into her suite without completely waking her. My father had a room and bathroom prepared with all of the basics she could need, including some stretchy yoga pants and small T-shirts. I figure I'll help her get some nicer things once we figure out her sizes and what she likes. This will do for her to recoup in though.

"Still sleeping?" Finn asks when I close her door and find him waiting right outside in the hall.

"Yeah, who knows the last time she was able to get some good rest. She's probably not used to having a full stomach like that too. You hungry?"

"A bit." He nods. "Could go for a drink and then bed myself."

"Was your room okay?"

"Your da did good. Yer sure he won't mind havin' me under his roof?"

"No, he's not in the Bratva anymore. Even if he were, you'd be welcome. You're my friend."

"That's not how it went awhile back."

"Well, that's how it goes with me involved. My father may have been a selfish prick before, but he's trying to make life simpler for me now."

He nods. And we come to the study where my dad's hanging up with someone on his cell.

"Sin." My father approaches, bringing back memories of hearing him speak to my mother and me in Russian when I was a boy.

"Victor." I greet, and he slightly winces. I think he's still holding out hope that one day I'll acknowledge him as my father to his face. "My good friend, Finn O'Kassidy." I gesture to the sturdy man beside me, and surprisingly my father grins holding his hand out to him next.

"Finn, you resemble your papa a great deal."

They shake hands, and Finn blinks a few times. "Thanks fer that."

His father's been dead for a long time, and mine just paid him a big compliment, welcoming him and speaking kindly of his father.

Victor nods. "Come join me for dinner, and you two can fill me in while we wait for the doctor to arrive and check over the little captive."

We head for the dining room that's been set with four places. To the side is many of my favorite dishes; Borscht which is a type of red sauce with pork and vegetables; Pelmeni which is meat filled dumplings; chicken kotleti which is ground chicken that's been breaded and sautéed; Syrniki which is a sweet pastry type of food, dusted with powdered sugar and raspberries; and, my father's favorite, Medovik which is essentially a honey cake. My mother has cooked these dishes many times while I was growing up.

"You've prepared." I acknowledge what he's offering. It would be rude not to, and with everything he's done recently to help gain his favor, he doesn't deserve for me to be disrespectful right now.

"Da." He stands behind the chair at the head of the table, his spot.

"Spaseeba."

He waves me off. "It's nothing. Anytime you wish to be here, I will prepare."

Finn and I sit on each side of him once Victor takes his seat—the empty plate left vacant beside me. "I didn't want to wake her." I don't want him thinking she's rude. He grew up in a different type of life, a different set of rules of what was expected.

"She's hurt, I do not take offense." He's been in Russia lately; I can hear it in the way he's speaking. His words and his English always change when he visits home. "Vodka?" he suggests, lifting the expensive bottle and pouring his glass half full.

"Da, spaseeba," I reply, nodding as he pours my glass, then he turns to Finn and pours his as well. It's customary in our family to always pour a guest's first glass of vodka to welcome them.

"You all fill your plates, and tell me what happened," he orders, and we comply. I'm starving. The private plane has decent food, but nothing like this.

Taking my seat again, I sip the delicious vodka and tell him all about our adventure and how I want to go back and kill each man responsible. As he listens to me speak passionately, I swear his shoulders grow wider and him taller as he sits, like he's about to burst with pride.

"You are my sin," he states proudly when we're finished talking about it, and you'd think it was Christmas morning the way he looks as he says it.

I'm his son, but I'll never be anything like him.

"You're gonna be happy," said life,

"but first I'll make you strong."

-quotags.net

Sasha

When I wake again, it's morning. At least it feels like morning and judging by the unfamiliar surroundings, I'm assuming we've made it to Beau's father's house. How out of it was I yesterday? I hope I didn't anger Beau and his father. I can't remember ever sleeping so long before or feeling this much energy. It reminds me of the few brief memories I have from being a little girl, always bouncing around.

An older lady enters the room quietly and smiles kindly at me when she notices my eyes open. She nods. "Miss."

Surely she can't mean me. I don't know what Beau told her for her to speak to me so respectfully. The Master's voice comes back to me, taunting as he's done so many times in the past. *You're nothing.* I'm nothing. I'm something to be bought and sold, used when needed and out of the way when I'm not.

No, he's not here. I won't let him command me when he's not my owner anymore. I belong to Beau now.

"Hello," I respond quietly.

"Bright day today. You should get some sun. Maybe Mr. Beau will take you for a walk," she suggests and opens the long, burgundy drapes, sunlight pouring in as she does. It's beautiful, the room, the light, her friendliness—all of it.

"If that's what he wants." I nod, and she smiles again.

"There are toiletries in your bathroom for you and a few items in the bureau for you to wear until Mr. Beau takes you shopping. It should get you through a few days while you recover. Did you need me to help you shower or dress?"

I've never had anyone help me do any of it before or offer to leave me alone to do it. I always showered quickly in cool water and dressed in my white gowns in front of the Master's men. It was required; they watched us all.

My arm's a little sore and still feels heavy, reminding me of the IV. I may need her help, after all, maybe that's why she's offered.

I glance down to find a small bright pink bandage in place, the tubes and needle gone.

"I patched you up last night once the drip was finished. The doc stopped by for a minute to look you over. He'll be back this afternoon or tomorrow to speak with you and do more." She pats her light grey hair as if it's messed up, but it's still pinned up in a perfect twist.

"I know how to wash myself."

"Okay dear, whenever you're ready then. I just want to make sure you can stand first. You may still be a little wobbly from the traveling." She comes to the bed and holds out a wrinkled, pale hand to me.

She's going to help? Why would she care if I need assistance?

Placing my hand in her steady grip, I climb to my feet, swaying a bit as my equilibrium plays catch-up. She remains beside me as I take a few careful steps, my hips also sore from my fall. It must've been fairly hard for me to feel the ache. Usually, I can block it out.

"I'm not weak usually. I promise I can be good help to you," I mumble as I slowly make my way to the attached bathroom.

"Honey, you're so frail, don't you worry your mind about being weak. You're a little fighter, bouncing back from a spell like that so quickly. Mr. Beau and Mr. Victor will be pleased when I let them know you've woken. You just take all the time you need; a warm shower will do you some good."

Her accent is heavy with a slow drawl to it. It reminds me of honey, sweet and thick.

"It'll be warm?" My gaze finds hers, and she nods, looking a touch sad after I ask. The words just left me without any thought. I couldn't help it. She said warm shower and my heart sped up — eager.

The bathroom is massive, reminding me of the Master's home. Everything was big there as well; only I was never allowed to use any of the fancy stuff. We all stayed in the basement there, in tiny cage-like rooms. I don't want to think of that though. I'm about to take my first warm shower in God knows how long — definitely since I was a child.

The lady lets go of my hand and reaches into the spacious shower, turning the water on for me and explains which button to push to increase the degrees and which to decrease it. She points out the different soaps and asks if I have a skincare regimen. I don't have any idea how to reply to that, so I remain quiet. By the time she leaves me, she looks quite sad, and I hate knowing that it was somehow my fault making her upset. I didn't do it on purpose; I wish she would've kept on smiling.

I say goodbye to the Chief and put my cell away. He was calling to tell me that Internal Affairs is one step closer to clearing me in the Johnson case. I'll believe it when I see it though. He also wanted to know why a field agent from the FBI had called his office hoping to speak to me.

It's pretty random that someone from their office would call me. Either they've noticed that I've been visiting my cousins lately and now my father, or else they have someone on the inside and they saw me at the events. Regardless, I don't want their attention from either one of those scenarios.

Chief gave me a number to return the call, but I'm not sure if I want to. Before digging myself in the middle of this sex trade business, I wouldn't have thought twice about talking to the FBI. Now, however, I know too much. I could answer too many questions if they were to ask them and that's not good.

It may also be time to get a new phone. I'm assuming they've been tracking mine. Not that I'm surprised; I know I'm tracked by the department lots of times. It's the fact that I know they're doing it and are open about it that puts me at ease. The FBI's sneaky, though. They like you to think they don't know who you are when in reality, they know everything about you and then some.

Then there's Finn. He's a criminal, but he's also my friend. He keeps his illegal activities away from me, and we're fine. I don't want anyone getting the impression I'm working with him in those aspects. In that same breath, I don't want any of Finn's associates, thinking he's turned rat to the cops. Rats die, and that's the last thing I want for him.

I'll figure it out. Let's hope whatever it is, doesn't send me to jail.

My knuckles rap against Sasha's door a few times before I push it open. Susan, my father's housekeeper, came down the stairs a little while ago pretty upset. She thanked me for helping Sasha and told me I have a kind heart. I don't know what happened; I didn't ask. I'll let Sasha fill me in on whatever she feels comfortable with. I don't want to break her trust already.

"Sasha?" I call as I step into the room. She's sitting dressed in her new yoga bottoms, white socks and a T-shirt with a towel wrapped around her hair, staring into the mirror. She looks to be in a trance. "Susan had mentioned about you being up for a walk outside today?"

Her careful gaze meets mine in the mirror. "You're not angry with me for the woman leaving?"

"About what?" I step farther into the room, coming to a standstill directly behind her.

We continue to speak while watching the other through the mirror and I like it, it feels like it makes her a touch braver and not as frightened to speak out of turn as yesterday. I'm hoping baby steps will bring her out of her shell. I noticed some fire in her at the first auction. It was brief, but it was there, and I want to bring it out again.

146

"The lady she seemed upset when she left here. She was nice. I didn't mean to make her sad, I promise."

Lightly, I place my hands on her shoulders, her striking eyes gazing at me, wide and hopeful. "You didn't do anything wrong. She just worries when people get injured or don't feel well. Are you hungry?"

"A little, you mentioned a walk?"

"Yes, we can do both if you have the energy. I don't want you to overdo it; you need rest."

"I'll be fine." She lifts her arms, wincing as she reaches for the towel wrapped hair.

"Woah." I gently place her hands in her lap. "Let me help you."

Taking the towel out, I tug it free gently, not wanting to pull her hair. Wet and freshly showered she's even more stunning. Her cheeks have a bit more color to them today as well. She's not so pale. She's also braless, and that has me clearing my throat and reciting misdemeanors and felonies in my mind to try and block out the arousing sight.

"Hand me the brush."

She does so immediately, grabbing the silver clad brush from the vanity in front of her and handing it to me over her shoulder. I lay the damp locks against her back and begin brushing from the bottom up. My mother used to let me do this when I was a little boy. She says it always made her feel cherished, and I also learned that women with long hair usually like to start at the bottom and work their way up. If not, it'll tangle up even more.

I brush for what seems like an hour, and my wrist is beginning to feel heavy from the strange position. Her hair was brushed out impeccably long ago, but the way she watched me in the mirror spurred me to keep going. How could I stop when she watched me so aptly, her expression relaxed and her eyes dreamy? I would've kept going if she asked me to.

"Ready?"

She nods, her lips turned into a tiny smile.

"Come on then." I hold my free hand out while setting the brush back down on the vanity. She places her palm in mine, rising to her feet, appearing much better than she had yesterday.

She stumbles just enough for me to wrap her in my arms securely. While her cheeks tint, part of me thinks it may have been on purpose. Could she have faked it so I'd hold her?

Her lips part as she gazes up at me and I have to clear my throat to speak. Damn it...there's that feeling from yesterday, again. I have to keep reminding myself that she's not here for me. She was hurt and most likely sexually abused for God knows how long. That's the real reason she's here; it doesn't matter if I want to kiss her. I can't.

"Are you okay? You're up for a walk?"

"Yes, thank you, Beau." Her voice is quiet, her eyelashes fluttering. She's beautiful and broken, and it's going to be hard keeping away from her. "I've not had anyone brush my hair since I was a little girl." Her gaze shoots to the floor, full of pain. Tenderly grabbing my hand, she leads the way toward the door.

When was the last time I just held hands with someone like this? My life is dangerous; it's not my place to drag a woman into it, so usually, I have some meaningless sex to scratch my itch. I can't remember ever holding their hands and talking randomly with them like this.

I don't want to be that way with Sasha, though. I want to hear everything there is to know about her—good and bad. Especially the bad, because I know it'll help fuel the burning rage festering inside and I'll put an end to Yema once and for all.

We stop by the dining room on our way out, and she tears up when she finds freshly made Syrniki with sliced strawberries on the buffet. Taking a few napkins, I load two for each of us on napkins so we can walk and snack. The sugar will help her with some energy. I want her to get some exercise but not overly exhaust herself. She's still incredibly weak even though she's too stubborn to admit it.

"Good?" I ask as we walk along one of the pebble-lined paths of my father's property, not wanting to bring up her reaction to the food. It's expansive, acres upon acres of wooded and grassy land. It reminds me of Viktor's, but without the small lake, he has behind his cabin.

"Divine."

"That's a strong word for a pastry." I grin, and she nods, smiling. "Were you always not allowed to speak?"

Her quietness has me intrigued and my mind going a million miles a minute trying to figure out what she's thinking. Women are usually chatty, but Sasha's quieter than some of the men I've been on missions with can be.

"It's not so much as we can't speak, but that we must be spoken to first. We must always be respectful and mindful of the men."

I grunt. Such horseshit these unrealistic expectations some of these dickhead men put on these women. "So there were more of you? The women from the events, they were there with you too?"

"Do I not please you?"

"Yes, of course, you do. That's not what I meant." She twists my words, taking them personally. It's not about not being happy with her; she'd intrigued me from the get-go. And then when she showed signs of possessiveness toward me at the auction, I was damn near hooked. Normally that sort of display turns me off in a woman, but after seeing her so tiny and no doubt broken, it was like watching a lion trapped inside a kitten ready to claw its way free.

"The other woman you bought is already gone, and you've asked Mr. Capelloni for a group of women. I have been unwell, but once I'm better, I can please you better than any of the others."

"You misunderstand my intentions, Sasha. Willow, the woman who left with me last weekend, has gone to my cousins to get well and be safe. Viktor, my cousin, has updated me, telling me that Willow is doing better and fitting in there nicely. I wasn't interested in her."

"You weren't? Then why spend so much money?" She continues to avoid my question about the other women. I need to find out if he always has a large group of women on hand. What he does to them and where he steals them from. I need to find Niko's sister and seek some sort of vengeance for all these women he's mistreated.

"Because the men in that place were making me sick. I had to save at least one woman that night and offer her a better life. Yema wouldn't give me you, so I took Willow."

"So, she is not yours then? Even with you giving her a name?"

"No." How can she not understand that I don't own women? She had to be around them for a long period of time to believe that idea is even acceptable. It's fucking ludicrous. "She's not mine, she never was. She's a free woman."

"Free..." It's whispered in awe. "Would the group of woman you buy be yours, then?"

"No. They would be free as well."

"And me?" She turns to me, stopping in the middle of the worn-down dirt pathway, eyes wide.

"You are free, too, Sasha. No one owns you." I expect happiness, joy, smiles, a hug, an excited yell—something to do with being happy over the fact she's no longer caged like a bird.

Tears begin to flow over her cheeks, her eyes sharp, staring at me full of betrayal. Only, I haven't betrayed her; I've rescued her. "How can you do this to me?" She cries, her bottom lip trembling and that move alone crushes my chest. I feel guilty, and I haven't harmed her at all, yet in her eyes I have.

"Baby?" I pull her to my chest, and she weeps into my shirt. She's so broken. I don't understand her question; it was spoken as an accusation. I didn't do anything to her but offer her freedom and a chance to be happy. "Why are you so sad?"

"I don't want to be free. I want to be yours." It's spoken so truthfully, yet so naïve. She has no idea what those words really mean, especially to a man like me. I may not be your average alpha that needs to beat on his chest to prove my worth, but if she were mine, she'd never belong to another, and I can't do that to her. She deserves to live a life and discover things outside of me.

"But you don't even know me, why would you want to belong to a man who you don't even know?"

"Because you were my *one*. The Master said someone would come for me, that it would be my turn, and then there you were. You were supposed to be him. What good am I if no one wants me?"

My body grows stiff, but I don't release her, offering her what comfort I can. The Master, whoever he is, is one fucked-up individual. It doesn't escape my notice that his name matches my last name. Would she freak out if I told her that little tidbit? I hate that I share anything with this menace of a being. And how can she possibly believe that no one wants her, that I don't want her? She's fucking beautiful. Even in this state, she's stunning. Everything she's been through, yet she's still so innocent inside, warped and bent to the will of a man who had no right to shape her in any way.

"Sasha, it's not that I don't want you, trust me. I've thought of kissing your lips several times in the past two days alone."

That does it. She leans away from my chest, and then she's on her tippy-toes, her mouth meeting mine. It completely takes me off guard, and I fumble for a moment to return the kiss. Her lips are soft and timid, but she still pushes forward, being brave in her own way, initiating our kiss.

She sucks my bottom lip between hers, and I pull back. This can't happen. I have to be the strong one. I'm met with more tears, falling from her eyes like raindrops.

"I can't, Sasha. Fuck, I'm sorry."

"Why not? You said there's nothing wrong with me."

"There isn't. Damn it; you're perfect. It's me, okay?"

"You?" She sucks in a deep breath and my thumbs wipe away the wetness under her eyes.

Ugh, my proclamation seems so stupid and cliché. I sound like a few of my buddy's on the force, never letting anyone too close, because of our line of work. I wish that were the only thing holding me back from her, but it isn't that simple. I hate this. In a different time, in a different world, perhaps she could be with me.

"Yes. I can't own you. I can't own anyone."

"Why? Please tell me why."

Maybe it's the way she asks so desolately, with her sweet voice. Maybe it's the guilt building inside of me. I don't know, but something sets it free. "Because..." I take a deep breath and release the truth, "...I'm a cop."

It comes out, and I can't believe I actually said the words. I've been around hardened criminals nearly my entire life and then going undercover, and I've never admitted anything. I've been beaten several times, in fights and around paranoid criminals seeking the truth, dying to know if I'm a cop. I lie and omit until it *becomes* my truth and whoever's around believes it. But put one petite and shattered woman in front of me with a few tears, and I cave, admitting my biggest secret.

Sasha

What do I say to that? How do I respond to him? He's a police officer. How is it even possible? His family is the Russian Mafiya. They would never let their soldiers go, let alone Mafiya royalty. I've been around the Master long enough to hear him speak about the loyalty of the Mafia man. That's exactly what Beau is when it's broken down—he's royalty. His family isn't just *in* the Mafiya; they run it. It's their blood that carries the name. Maybe he is a corrupt officer like the ones Yema and the Master bring to visit us sometimes. That would make sense. Maybe it's a part of their plan? It's hard to think of anything bad when it comes to Beau, though. He doesn't fit the part from what he's shown me so far.

"I know a few officers," I admit reluctantly. I'm not supposed to ever speak of the men I've met before. There's something about Beau that makes me want to share everything with him. I want to make him like me, and if this is the only way, then I'm not above spilling my secrets if it brings him to me. He did, after all, admit to me his own secret. That has to mean something, right?

"You know them how?" he asks, leading me back toward the large estate. It's even bigger than the Master's home. People are nice here, though, which makes a huge difference.

My forehead scrunches. I don't think he really wants the answer to that question. He may not look at me so kindly if I tell him. Maybe I should've kept my mouth closed about it. I just want his attention on me and no one else. Who cares about the other officers or the other women.

My stomach's still fluttering from the kiss. I can't believe I did it and he didn't punish me. Maybe he likes the more forward women? If he gives me a little time, I'll learn what he likes, and I'll do everything I can to become it. I know he said he couldn't own me, but that's never stopped men before. I can see the kindness in his gaze, and I want that for myself. So many of the others have gone to men that are full of hate and violence. Beau isn't that man, and I want him to keep me. I want to be the lucky woman who captures him in my own way.

"We shouldn't speak about this anymore."

"Don't clam up on me now. You admitted that you know a few cops. I want to know how and who they are."

"Th-they visited the Master's home a few times," I admit, not wanting to go into further detail, but Beau's not one to give up so easily when it comes to information I've discovered.

"To arrest him?"

"No." I shake my head, hoping it'll be the end of the questioning as we take the steps to enter the house.

"They were acquaintances?"

Why must he be so persistent? "They were there to see a few of the women."

"You included?"

My gaze shoots to the ground as I nod my head again. I don't want to see his look of disgust when I admit the truth to him. The officers weren't so kind, threatening horrible things if we didn't obey them.

His hand goes to my cheek, pulling my face toward him. "You did nothing wrong, Sasha. I need you to tell me everything you remember though. You don't have to do it right this very moment, but eventually, I need to know. And any names you can recall would be really helpful, locations too."

"I'll tell you what I know." *But not what they did.*

We're interrupted by his father. He's scary, but still handsome like his son and appears much more serious. He has some graying at his temples and a clean-shaven face. He's a very well put together man.

"There you two are." His eyebrows rise at Beau's hand still on my cheek, a look of intrigue crossing his face.

"Victor." He acknowledges and drops his hand to envelope mine. "Come on, Sasha, we'll finish that conversation a little later, okay?" "Okay." I send a small smile toward his father. "Mr. Masterson."

He chuckles, amused. "Oh no, young lady. I don't use that fake name. I stick to my Russian roots. I'm too proud for that nonsense. Besides, Beau answers to Masters anyhow. You may call me Victor."

My breath catches in my throat.

Masters?

"It's to help keep my identity safe since I'm a cop," Beau interrupts, catching my surprise and shooting a scowl at his father.

"Beau Masters?" I ask, rolling the name over my tongue and deciding I like the way it sounds. It's strong, like the man himself. I don't so much care for the last name, but I know he's nothing like the man who tormented me.

"Yes. Although that's not even close to his real last name. You go to Russia; men would tremble if they heard his true name." Victor shakes his head and leads his way inside.

I can imagine if his father has been the one to name him and spread the word. I love my country, but many of the men from there are merciless, hardened beings. Not sure I can really compare them to the Sicilians that had kept me for so many years though. They'll always be terrifying to me after making my mother disappear.

"This isn't Russia. This is America, and my name is Beau Masters. I haven't answered to anything else since I was a child." It's spoken with a touch of venom and finality, and I can't help but wonder why he speaks to Victor with such hostility and disrespect.

Men are confusing. If I were to speak to him like that, I'd most likely end up buried or burned in some field. I don't get it why you'd want to treat your parents like that anyhow. My mother was everything to me. She was so beautiful and kind; I'd do anything to be able to tell her I love her.

"What are you thinking, little dove?" Beau gives my hand a brief squeeze.

"That I wish I could tell my mother that I love her."

Victor's step falters, and Beau's gaze grows stunned. "You have a family?" He asks like the thought never even flitted through his mind. I'm an auctioned woman, a nothing. Why would anyone expect me to have family—a sister, a mother, a father, or anyone for that matter, who'd love or want me? Men are selfish beings.

"Yes, of course, my mother. Only I'm confident she's dead. I think she died the day I was taken."

"And when was that, young lady? Do you remember?" Victor stares at me with kindness and curiosity, shedding the scariness from before as we come to the plush sitting room.

Rich men and their fancy rooms. I'm sure he has a spotless bar around here somewhere too. It's not a bad thing, but not only are men selfish, but they're creatures of habit too.

"I was only a girl. Probably six years or around there, I cannot be sure. I can't remember it all; it's a bit fuzzy."

Beau sucks in a quick breath, letting it back out through his clenched teeth, his hands clamped in tight fists. I don't know why he'd be upset about it, though. I can't remember, that should be a good thing, I think?

"They had you for that long? The Master or whatever the fuck his name is?" Ah, I understand his anger. If he only knew just how many children get taken, it's much more than he'd expect.

"The Master, again?" Victor grumbles, familiar with the name.

Beau nods shortly.

"My dear, you don't mean Don Franchetti, do you? There are rumors that's what his girls call him. Forgive me; it's been a while since I've been around any of them."

"I'm sorry, I do not know his name. We were told to call him Master and Mr. Capelloni, except in public. Then Mr. Capelloni is just Yema. They like to be casual at the auctions and formal when away from everyone."

"I see." Victor sighs, pouring himself a glass of something clear. Beau tugs me lightly to sit on the sofa next to him. It's fancy with pretty grey material trimmed with wood along the bottom. "I got a call this morning, Beau; Viktor will be here either this evening or tomorrow."

"He's coming here?"

"Yes, he wants to meet Sasha and discuss your plan to move forward with the others."

"Okay. I'm just surprised to hear he's okay with coming here and doesn't want me to go to him."

He sighs again, clearly feeling every bit of his age. "I told him he was welcome, but to leave Tatkiv at home. I'm not in the mood to deal with my brother's wild child. Viktor is always welcome; I'll stay away if you two wish when you speak about business."

"Tatkiv?" I turn to Beau.

He nods. "It's my cousin Tate. Tate is short for Tatkiv. He has like three or four different names he answers to. His father did that when he was younger so fewer people would know who he is. Figured it'd keep him safer that way being so close to the organization."

"Oh. Like the Master?"

"Yes, we know he has another name, but not his real name. It makes it harder for us to find out who he really is. And Viktor is Tate's brother, they're both my cousins."

"That makes sense. Will you ever tell me your real name? The one you were born with?"

"Maybe someday." His mouth tilts down a touch, obviously not too fond of it. He's lucky, though at least he knows his real name. I'm still confused if Sasha is mine from my mother or the Master. I should know it, but after so long, it's hard to remember. I learn to answer to whatever they call me, and most of the time it was just girl.

"Is Mr. O'Kassidy leaving today?" his father asks, breaking Beau's intense stare on me.

"Yeah, he has to get back to his business, you know how it is."

"Will you have protection at the next event then, without him here?"

"Yeah, Finn said he'll come with me next time too, or else I have the men Viktor sent with me. I'll be fine."

"Good. It makes me proud to see you close with your cousins, working with them. Be sure to let Susan know when you're ready for lunch and she'll take care of you. I'm going to make a call to the doctor now that Sasha is up and moving around. We want her on the quickest road to recovery."

"Spaseeba," he replies, and Victor leaves the room, foregoing his glass tumbler. I love hearing them speak Russian, even if it's just random bits. It reminds me of being home.

"They speak Italian so we can't understand them," I say out of the blue, remembering a small detail and thinking it might be helpful.

"You're certain it's Italian?"

"Yes, when I was a child, the Master would let me ask questions sometimes and one thing I asked was what language they spoke. It didn't seem familiar to me. The Master told me it was Italian so I couldn't understand them. He spoke to us in English. We all learned English because he said most men that would buy us would come from America or else speak English. The men I saw were from everywhere though. I think they told us that so we would never know what they were talking about."

"That makes sense. There are plenty of times we'll speak Russian too, so others don't understand us as well."

"It reminds me of home; I enjoy hearing you."

"Yeah? Are you really Russian? That wasn't something Yema threw up there for the show?"

"No. I am Russian. It's one of the few things I'm sure of."

"If you give me your mother's name, I can see if I can locate her for you."

Beau offering to find her for me is the nicest thing anyone has ever done. Not giving me food or medicine or clothes or even sleep. To know he's kind enough to find my mother only makes me want to belong to him even more. I wish I still had a mother alive to find, but I know she's gone. I'd still feel her warmth if her heart was beating.

"You are the sweetest, Beau." I smile and lean over, kissing his cheek. He pulled away from my kiss earlier, but I can't stop myself from kissing him in some way. Is it wrong that I want to touch him? I don't usually care for it, but his tenderness has me wanting to be close to him. How can you not want to express gratitude to someone like him?

"You have to stop doing that, Sasha," he scolds softly, as if he wants it to happen but has to say these things.

"Why?" My muscles grow stiff. He's kind yet won't let me touch him. He'll hold my hand, but won't let me kiss him. He lets me talk freely and ask questions, yet he holds back. I know I shouldn't expect anything from him, but men like to touch me. Why doesn't he? Why is he so confusing?

"Because I already told you we can't do this." His head shakes, and it causes my chest to clench tightly.

"No, I can't do this!" I respond in a sad huff, tears pooling in my eyes. He's already seen me cry. I don't want to be weak in front of him anymore. He allows me to speak to him however I wish, and it's strange, but refreshing, not bottling my frustrations up completely like I'm used to. Standing, I turn away. "I'm tired."

It's a lie. I can't handle him pushing me away anymore right now. The denial, the detachment, hurts too badly coming from someone like him.

"I'll walk you to your room so you can rest."

Ever the gentleman, he makes it even worse by offering.

"Thank you, but I don't want to push you any further. I can find my way," I reply stubbornly and leave out of the

164

sitting room as quickly as I can. It's not very fast with my sore thigh and tired body, but I do the best I can to appear strong in front of him. I can cry in the room I'm staying in without him seeing me confused and upset. He's seen me weak enough already.

I was nearly asleep when my bed covers shift, the mattress dipping under pressure from a petite body sliding into the bed with me. It has my muscles wound tight, as people aren't normally able to sneak up on me so easily. I must've been leaning more toward being asleep than I'd thought for me not to hear the door open or click as it closed. That's not good. I have to stop letting myself get too tired to stay alert, even in sleep.

"What are you doing?" My voice is loud and gruff out into the silent night.

"I wanted to lay with you." Her voice is soft…meek and has my groin tightening with lustful thoughts.

"You shouldn't be in here."

"Please let me stay; I won't bother you. My room is much bigger than the space I'm used to. I've never been alone so much before."

Christ and she begs me; it'll cripple a man's resolve quick.

Fuck. I didn't even think of that; I assumed she'd want as much privacy as possible. It turns out I was wrong — again.

"Okay," I reply absently, acutely aware of her presence in my bed, merely a foot away from me. She's making it harder and harder to keep up with my resolve. I could so easily touch her right now, and in the middle of the night when I'm full of sleepiness, it has my defenses down even more. I can't hold myself back from her heat if she comes at me. I'm afraid I'll be too harsh or else give in completely.

"Are you all right?" I ask after a moment of tense silence. I feel like I could cut the tension with a knife, she has my body so wound up.

"Yes, Beau; I like it better in here."

I hold back the groan of hearing my name leave her lips. I'm a fucking dog for thinking of her this way. "Good. Night, Sasha."

"Goodnight, Beau." She yawns and snuggles into my side.

It's going to be the longest night of my life, keeping myself from touching her like I dreamt about since I first laid eyes on her.

It becomes our nightly routine for three straight weeks until I'm called back into work and am forced to fly back home to California. The funny thing is, when I got there, I realize that I hadn't missed it like I normally do when I'm away. It was nice to drive my Jeep, but the apartment was just that. It didn't feel like home. The East is beginning to call to me more and more. My family, the humidity...ahh, hell, the girl...

I put in for leave and lie to my chief about my father being sick and needing to stay in Tennessee longer. He doesn't hesitate to approve it because he trusts me. He knows I wouldn't normally ask unless it was important. More lying and now to my boss, a man I respect. When did my life become this, where I'd rather be on this side of the fence than the other?

Two more weeks of getting time with her and two more weeks to try and stop this sex trafficking that's so widely accepted by the various crime families. If only time were in my favor.

"We have to stop, Sasha," I grumble against her mouth as I pull away from her. She snuggled into me, and I couldn't help myself. When her head tilted up to me, reflecting in the moonlight, my lips met hers on their own accord. My resolve dissipated with that one look from her. She's wearing me thin—a man can only hold off for so long.

I was gone back to Cali for two days to take care of work. I missed having her snuggled up to me every night. My body's grown used to sharing a bed with her and the past two nights I barely slept a wink, tossing and turning. She consumed my thoughts the entire time. I know I'm becoming too close to her, but no matter how many times I scold myself, I pull her right back to my body when I'm with her.

Now it seems as if my body wants even more from her, the sleeping beside her, not merely enough to satiate my cravings for her warmth. My mind knows I shouldn't be doing this. I've been around her here at my father's for three weeks, slowly chipping away at her layers and she's fucking magnificent. Utterly beautiful and kind on the inside, as well as the outside and it's dangerous. She can easily become my undoing, my weakness, my downfall. I need to be the one to protect her, to save her.

I was going to go back to work for a while and save up more vacation time. But then my father called me the first night I was away, telling me that Sasha was refusing to eat with me gone. Naturally, I became extremely worried, especially the next morning when Victor called me yet again saying she'd turned away breakfast. Her body doesn't need to have her causing more harm to it by refusing to feed it the nutrients it's lacked for God knows how long. It's amazing she survived as long as she did. I doubt they gave the women regular medical care or anything like that.

I knew I needed to get back here ASAP. She ate dinner with us this evening thankfully, even if it wasn't much. My father's still furious over it all, but it was a start, and I'm grateful she relented.

She'll eat again in the morning, I promised him. If not, he wants to bring the doctor in again and look at other options. She won't like those, but then no one would enjoy being force-fed I imagine.

The last thing I want is for someone poking and prodding, making her uncomfortable. She's been through enough. Obviously, I'd just left her alone too soon. My father and Susan are here, but they aren't much when it comes to company. It doesn't bother me much, as I'm used to the solidarity, but Sasha is used to a constant presence. Everything was always mapped out for her, and now she has this sort of free reign. I didn't understand at first, but now I get it, that it could be overwhelming having all these choices to make out of nowhere.

"I don't want to stop. I want you close," she urges, her voice husky with need. My mouth meets hers, this time even hotter as her velvety tongue swirls with mine, tangling in a delicious mating dance. My hands weave into her blonde locks that've grown shinier with her time here, and her delicate palms find my bare chest.

We kiss for what feels like forever, and I pull myself away from her again. I have to stop it now, or else there'll be no turning back. I'll take her, and I'll regret it in the morning. I'd love every moment of being with her, of feeling her intimately, but I know she'll think of me like all the others and that thought alone I can't stand. I have to be different; she has to know inside that she deserves better.

"Shh…enough, Sasha. Sleep, moy baby."

My lips breeze over her forehead in a chaste kiss, and I turn my body away from her. Giving her my back is the safest option right now for the both of us. My cock's so flipping hard I'm liable to poke my eye out if I'm not careful. I don't want her discovering me so turned on. I don't want to make her uncomfortable in any way. If this were to ever happen and that's a big if, she'd have to be one hundred percent sure it's what she wanted. I'm nothing in this; it's all her and what she's comfortable with. I refuse to cheapen her or make her feel used in any way. I won't be like anyone from her past. She deserves so much better than that. Until that point, if it ever comes, she needs a goddamn chastity belt to keep my cock in check.

The memories and information she's shared over the past few weeks makes me sick inside for her. I don't treat her any differently because of them either. I think she was afraid that I would, but if anything I look at her with more awe than I had before.

How a woman can survive such a hellish life is beyond me. She's broken, but she's also so damn strong, and one day she'll figure that out. Those men—if you can even call them that—broke her, but she lived and prevailed. I'll see the end to them one way or another if it's the last thing I can do for her.

Eventually, I drift off to sleep, but not sure for how long. It feels like I've merely closed my eyes, but it must've been longer for sleep to be filling me so strongly. I'm on my back, my boxers are down, and there's a hand wrapped around my length, steadily working me over.

So good—so fucking good—is what it is.

I'd almost believe it was a dream if I couldn't feel her excited breaths against my ribs, turning me on even more. Her head is resting on my side, right next to my abs, so fucking close to my groin; I feel like I'm vibrating. She has my body so heated with pent-up need. Even my toes are curled. Asleep or not, my body certainly responds to her touch. She could own me if she wanted, if she pushed me enough.

"What are you...?" I say gruffly into the night, trying to clear my head enough to process everything and think rationally. That's not happening, though; she has me floating on cloud nine.

"Shhh." She responds in the same fashion I do to her so often, her breath blowing over my stomach even more as her hand grips me, moving up and down in a rhythmic circle.

She just shushed me, and she's jerking my cock like she's trying to milk me or something. I'm going to spill everywhere if she keeps it up, twisting me deliciously.

Her motions are determined, and I feel the need building inside me like a volcano. I've been yanking on my dick every day for the past three weeks like a man possessed and none of those times felt remotely close or as good as right now with her doing it. At one point I was afraid of getting friction burn, or that I'd eventually tug on the fucker so much, it'd stop working. It undeniably works right now. She's not having any difficulty getting me to stand at attention, saluting her.

It's working so well, in fact, that I'm nearly ready to explode. After wanting her for so long, my calf's tense up and I feel as if I could shoot to the ceiling.

"Baby, I'm gonna come if you don't stop that."

At my words, her head drops below the blanket draped across my abdomen, and her hot little mouth wraps around the head of my cock. It's like a goddamn eruption. Just one powerful suck from her vacuum grip lips and I'm coming so much; I'm afraid she'll choke on it. What's more

172

impressive is her swallowing every drop I have. A loud groan leaves me, rumbling from my chest in pure bliss.

I don't even know what to say. I feel like I got overly excited and just came in five minutes. Not very impressive on my part, but no doubt mind-blowing on hers.

"Now I can go to sleep." She sighs, placing tender kisses on my stomach. If she's not careful, she'll wake the beast again, only this time a quick tug job won't do it. It takes some long, hard fucking to get rid of that one and if it doesn't happen, I'll damn sure not be getting a wink of sleep.

I fall asleep, still panting, mind blissed out.

She wakes me like this for a week straight, *every single night*. She not only climbs into bed next to me but wraps her hot little mouth around my length, waking me in the most delicious way. And each night she won't let me touch her. Fuck, if I don't want to. She has me thinking about her each waking moment of the day and then dreaming about her when I close my eyes at night. I'm enraptured with her every move, her every thought she shares with me.

It's beyond frustrating; I want to feel her all over and bring her pleasure too. But I get it. I don't really, I never will, but I'm patient, and I'll stay that way as long as needed. Doing everything she wants, not like I can hold myself back at this point, things have changed. Our relationship's grown, evolving into a friendship with an attraction so strong I'm sure it'll light the sheets on fire one night.

Each day she eats, and we go for our walk, and as the days pass, she grows more beautiful, more outspoken with me. She essentially blooms in front of my eyes, and I'm coming to the conclusion that at the end of this whole thing, I don't think I'm going to be able to let her go and that makes me a fucking bastard. She doesn't deserve to be a kept woman; she deserves more—freedom. I want her freedom to be with me, one of these nights my feelings tipped past the point of return.

Now, I not only want justice for the men doing these horrifying things, but I want to become dark. I want to become so fucking twisted I hurt them for what they've done to Sasha. The others matter, but I'm falling for her and so help me, I don't want the law to take care of this one, this time. I want to do it; I want to dole out my own punishment for crimes committed.

It's Friday again, and she begs me not to go, but I do. I leave her to become closer to the men I want to hurt, and I get out of the God awful auction with seven women this time. Yema's growing comfortable with me, though it takes everything in me not to put a bullet in his skull just yet. It'll happen; I just have to remain patient for the time being.

Sasha's upset, refusing to eat the entire three days I'm gone again, and I feel like I'm going to detonate, being pulled in so many directions. She's worried for my safety that I'll find another. She begs me on my father's phone with tears, and it's like twisting a knife in my stomach. The last thing I want is her upset or not doing well.

She's needy and fuck if I don't love every minute of it. I know it's not healthy, but I love having a broken little bird waiting for me. Letting me be the only one who saves her. It's sick, but a sane man can't work undercover next to criminals each day and not become tainted in some ways.

"Sasha, calm down, I'm back." I've barely briefed my father over what happened on my latest trip, and now I'm dealing with her wrath. She's in a mood to argue, my sweet woman I saved who would barely speak in the beginning is ready for a fight.

"You'll go again; you realize they'll kill you the moment they find out who you really are?"

"They know who I am, we've been over this."

"They know the story you tell them, nothing else. If they discover you're really a cop and not the dirty kind, I'll never see you again." Her concern for me is heartwarming, but I've taken care of myself for many years now.

"Even if they did find out, clearly I'm not completely innocent; I've been buying women from them for Christ's sake. They would believe me to be flipped."

"I'll tell them." She stands stubbornly, and my temper ignites like gasoline poured on fire. After all I've done, she grows ballsy enough to throw threats around.

"The fuck you will. I can handle myself. You'll do as you're told and stay here, stay safe!"

"No." She shakes her head, tears dripping off her chin. "I'll find a way to let them know so you can't go back."

"You do that, and you condemn all those helpless women to a life of hell. Why protect them? That's all you'll be doing."

"I don't care about any of them, and maybe that makes me terrible, but I only care about you. Those men—they're evil. There's so much you don't know they do, you could never be as horrible as they are."

"They kill people? Guess what Sasha, so have I. That's the whole reason why I was off work when I first met you; I'd killed someone. I'm not an innocent man by any means. I told you I don't work regular jobs. This shit going on is vile, but I can handle it. You need to trust me to take care of everything."

"They'll hurt you."

"Mafiya blood runs through my veins. Do not underestimate me," I scowl, growling the words sternly and her eyes flair.

She's on me a second later, feeling lighter from her stubbornness of not eating the entire weekend. It's amazing she has this much fire in her. Her lips meet mine, and it's like finding home. The kiss isn't sweet or gentle; it's angry, needy, and consuming.

She bites at my lips, and I can only take so much, tossing her on the bed and peeling my shirt over my head. I stalk toward the bed, unclasping the button on my jeans. This is so far overdue; my cock could break through concrete at this point.

"You shut your mouth, threatening me. You don't know what kind of a man I am." I yank her foot toward me and start pulling her yoga pants down her legs. Rather than scaring her as I'd expect, she pants, her cheeks red with desire. Her chest moves with her heaving breaths, lips slightly parted, making her the most gorgeous woman I've ever seen.

"What are you doing?" she asks breathily, the tears dried up as she watches me shove my pants from my hips and then rip her panties off. They're plain black, nothing special, but she's the type to make clothes sexy, not the other way around.

Grabbing her other ankle, I yank her even closer. Her ass is resting on the edge of the bed, my cock in line with her lips as I tug her T-shirt off next. She's not wearing a bra, and my dick gets even bigger if that's possible. Of course, it's possible. Who are we kidding? My cock's anything but small.

"You want me to show you that I'm powerful, that I can fuck you better then all those other men? Don't challenge me, Sasha, I'll fucking ruin you for everyone else," I declare, and she responds softly, meeting my gaze.

"You already have."

Screw having my cock sucked, her pussy's the only thing that'll satisfy me at this point. I just hope she's ready inside.

Pushing her down, her back meets the bed, and I lean over, sliding into her and shoving her farther back onto the bed with my hips. The drive's powerful and I can hear her suck in a breath.

"Is this what you need? You need my cock deep inside, so you'll shut that mouth up? You need to feel how big I am to show you I'm a strong man?"

"I know you're strong, but I am not," she whispers against my throat, peppering kisses against the scruff.

"Oh but baby, you are and so, so stubborn."

I pull her legs over my shoulders and go to town, fucking her like it's my dying wish. She loves having me take control like this. I don't mind it in the bedroom, but outside, I don't want to control her.

Obviously, this is something I'm assuming she needs after being controlled nearly her entire life. Of course, it's a turn on to her. She knows I'd never actually hurt her. At least I hope she does.

"You know I'd never hurt you, right?" I ask as she moans into my neck.

"I know, Beau, I know." She nips and sucks the skin on my chest, driving my desire a level higher. She's pure bliss, her body taking mine like it can't get enough.

It's not enough; my palm flies into her hair, yanking backward until her face tilts up and I can bite onto her chin. It makes her moan again, and I thrust forward over and over in and out of her wet heat. She's divine like chocolate custard, on a sunny day full of laughter. That's what I feel whenever she's near, and being inside her only amplifies it. My place in Cali isn't home, she is.

"I'm falling for you, Sasha." The words spill from me as I let my guard down for her and her alone. It could be my downfall at this rate. She drives me crazy with feelings, with lust, with want, with need. I should shut up before I admit to something that I'm not ready for. Hell, I'm sure she isn't ready for all of that either.

"I'm yours, Beau," she calls out as my cock begins to throb.

Reaching between us, I find the tiny nub of pleasure between her thighs. One hand braced next to her shoulder and the other rubbing circles, pinching softly, squeezing just enough to make her hips buck.

"You remember I will protect you and myself." It's a statement, no more debating; she'll get it if I have to fuck it into her. "No more questioning me, Sasha," I demand as I pinch her clit and she screams, her pussy grabbing onto my cock like a vice.

"You understand me?" Fuck, I hope she gives in, I'm about to blow out the side of her pussy with how badly I need to come.

"Yes-yes, just let me…"

She trails off as my thumb presses down, and I grind my hips into her as she screams with her release. A loud groan leaves me as I pump into her furiously, cum spilling from my dick like it can no longer hold back, coating her insides with my seed.

"You're mine."

"I'm yours," she admits, and my mouth takes hers in a searing kiss. I kiss her until my cock's heavy again, but this time, I take it slow and worship her like the goddess she truly is.

Hours pass before I pull her to my chest completely sated. Kissing her forehead tenderly, still thinking of the feelings bursting through me at finally being this intimate with her and she sleeps like it's the first time she's been able to in God knows how long. My guess would be three days.

Find your tribe,

love them hard.

-Danielle LaPorte

Sasha

He's finally back. Something happens to me when he leaves. My body and mind sink into a desolate gloom, knowing what I do about the men he's around and what it is he's doing there. The Master will figure out Beau's plan. He's a smart man, and then they'll take him away from me. My one saving grace and they'll kill him; I know it, and I can't let that happen no matter what.

I need to go with Beau to the next auction; I'll be able to help. I wasn't fond of him around the other women, but now that I'm certain he's not keeping any of them, I want to do whatever I can. That sounds completely selfish and unkind of me, but I have to look out for myself first. None of them would've thought twice about helping me if they got away from that place of torment. Living around the Master and his men is rough; it's not so much living, but mostly just existing and trying not to anger any of them. Their taunts and punishments can be brutal if you step out of line.

The majority of them left me alone. I knew what was expected and they were aware that I didn't belong to them, so they barely spoke to me. In fact, it's as if they avoided me, most likely frightened to have an exchange with me that wasn't ordered by their boss. Some of them took my body, but it was a gift from the man himself, an offering when his men had done something worthy in his eyes. I learned to turn it all off, just block it out and think of happy stories when they overtook my body. I had to relent, but in no way would I let them have my mind as well. I was keeping that for myself.

In a way, I grew to love the Master. It sounds strange, but he kept me alive for many years, and I'm not that naïve to know that my life could've been so much worse than it was.

There were many women that died. They were killed trying to escape or who would lash out and then they'd be burned as if they were a witch at the stake like they meant nothing. They were treated like animals and disposed of quickly.

Yes, he hurt me, but I learned. I became invisible once I was no longer a child and he wasn't amused with me any longer. I helped the cook whenever it was possible. She took a kindness to me, offering me scraps and water. It was enough to survive on. It's a man's world, and I became the perfect shell, always seeking to please them whether it was me remaining silent or on my knees gazing at them as if they hung the moon.

And I hated the Master in the same breath. I hated them all, but I shoved it all down, locked it away. There's no time to have a reckless emotion such as hate eating you up inside when you have to survive when you have to be perfect or risk an unfathomable wrath. Hate is like poison, slowly killing you one black mass at a time.

I wasn't going to let it ruin me, so I grew thankful for each day I persevered. I'd been there for many years; I was one of the longest, along with the maids and cooks. They were like me; they did their jobs and stayed in line, never missing a beat. That's why I'm certain Beau needs me to help him free the others. I'm the only one who knows as much as I do. It's unbelievably hard to think of everything and to have to share it with him, but if it helps him stop them, well then, I'll do it.

The only real empathy I felt for the others is when I'd see the little girls come in. It made me depressed inside, throwing me back into memories I'd worked hard to bury in the back of my mind. Those are the people I'm thinking of now. The young girls, torn from their parents' arms as they walk down the streets, the ones whose lives have merely begun. The untainted and the innocent.

I wish someone would've been there to save my mother and me. There's nothing I can do about that now, but maybe help bring someone's daughter home to them. I have to convince Beau to let me go with him.

That night I crawl into his bed, loving the warmth his body radiates. It's like his soul calls to mine, beckoning me closer, to want and need him. I've never felt the pull like this around anyone else, and it's intoxicating as if I can't be near him enough.

His body makes me feel alive, and his words fill me with hope again. The only thing that worries me besides his safety is figuring out how to make him keep me. He's like a puzzle, so many pieces that are being put together but one piece at a time.

He's awake as my naked form straddles over top of him. Last night was blissful, him taking me like I belong to him. In a sense he made me his, whether he wants to admit that's what it was or not, it's the truth. He brought me so much pleasure too. It'd always been about the men in the past, but Beau gave me the impression it was to make me feel good. My body's been humming all day, waiting for the moment his defenses would be down, and I could share in his warmth again.

"We shouldn't do this." He greets me with the same gruff, sleep-laden voice and declaration as all the nights prior. I don't care if we shouldn't, he fills my heart, and that's what matters to me. He's always worried about doing what he believes is the right thing, but I want him to forget his thoughts and get lost in me.

"Shhh." My fingers fall to his lips as my hips rock over his, enticing him to seat himself deep inside of me again.

It does the trick, and a pleased grumble rumbles through his chest. His hands land on his groin, pushing the boxer briefs down enough to free his length. Beau's glorious in that department; huge would be the word I'd use to describe his cock.

His skillful fingers find my entrance, filling me until my head grows fuzzy and I can think of nothing else but having him completely. He turns me into this wanton creature, aroused and dizzy in the best sort of way.

"Please," I keen, lightly running my nails along his muscular torso.

His body is beautiful, so many colors from the tattoos smothering his skin. It reminds me of when I was young, and I'd spend hours coloring in my books. I always loved lots of colors, never having only one favorite. His tattoos are the same, colors upon multiple shades, swirling over his tan flesh. He's like a canvas hung somewhere spectacular so you can stare and ponder what everything could possibly mean. I wonder what stories his ink tells, and if he'd share them with me some day.

"You want this, little dove?"

"Yes. I want you, Beau, so badly."

The words work like magic, and on the next breath, he's inside me, filling me so wonderfully. His strong grip finds my hips next and anchors me to him, rocking and tilting my body in so many ways. Each movement brings satisfying pleasure along with an insatiable need, both of us wanting, craving every last bit we have to offer each other.

At this rate, I may never get my fill of him. He admitted he's falling for me. They were probably the most glorious words I've heard escape his lips.

His moans drive me on, his grip keeping me secure, making me feel cherished and safe. He'd never let anyone hurt me ever again, and it makes me want to worship him, forfeit everything to those remarkable hands of his. He's easily overtaking my soul, staking its claim as his.

"You're stunning." The words escape his lips with a low grunt. My wetness between my thighs admits just how much I love hearing his voice, his proclamations while we're wrapped up in each other.

"I want more." I can't believe the request comes from me, but he has my world quickly spinning out of control, his body casting a spell of sorts over mine. He does this to me, freeing my thoughts and feelings. And I never feel ashamed or out of place around him either.

"You'll have everything." He leans up, taking my breasts into his mouth, switching from one to the other back and forth, sucking, nipping, and pleasuring them. His hand, trails over my heated flesh to my core, his expert fingers, circling, pressing and pulling on the tiny part controlling so much of my desire.

His movements have moans spilling from me like a waterfall, bliss knocking on my door, pushing me over the cliff of fulfillment. He does this — no other man — only him. He plays me like a violin in the sweetest song, serenading my will to his want.

"That's it, fuck yes." He groans against my chest, still lapping at my breasts like a man depraved, as his cock grows firmer, pulsing inside my center. It's like a volcano, nearly ready to erupt, building up more and more pressure as he knocks me into another orgasm. The feeling's so extreme, my head falls forward. My hands clutch his shoulders like a steely vice, holding on for dear life as I ride him into oblivion.

Moments fade into minutes, slowly becoming more as I tilt and swirl, moaning and calling for him. The sex morphs into a sultry dance between two beings, gyrating to and from, back and forth. Our bodies seek and search the other out and when we find each other, fusing like we belong to the other. Only then do we reach a new level of satisfaction — a new level of understanding, of devotion.

He's mine, and I'm undoubtedly his.

The next morning comes along faster than I'd like and his cousin Viktor along with it. I met him briefly the last time he'd visited and he scared me. He reminds me so much of the Master, it made my stomach sick inside. He wasn't evil toward me, but I could tell he was strict—a man who rules over many others.

He and Beau are more than family I noticed. They're close, like a friend or brother would be I'd imagine. I don't really know, not having any of my own, but that's what I'd think it'd be like.

After showering, I pull on my plain T-shirt and another pair of yoga capris. I go about filling myself with false bravado and courage to face Viktor, Beau, and his father for brunch. One of them isn't so bad, but all three of them together makes me a bit squeamish inside with anxiety.

I wind my way through the vast hallways lit by crystal sconces along the walls until I descend the overzealous staircase. Everything is supersized it seems. The Master's house was big, but this place reminds me of a castle.

I understand why Beau would want to be here rather than his apartment in California. He explained it's much smaller than here and we wouldn't be comfortable. If he could've seen the space I stayed in before, he'd know this house is what fairy tales are made of. I slept on a small mattress on the floor. He has no idea the life he's given me so far. I would be grateful of anything just because of the way he treats me.

Eventually, I end up at the smaller dining area reserved for breakfast and lunch. Rich people are so strange needing so many different rooms to eat in. The space is stunning and a bit more modern compared to the formal dining room that's used for dinner. The table in here is made up of thick glass and seats eight in a huge circle. The table and chairs are positioned directly in front of an enormous window that overlooks the gorgeous property out back that's been landscaped with so many flowers it could supply a florist if needed.

The spread along the glass top is far too much food for twenty people to eat, let alone the four people here, myself included. And there's orange juice. I've discovered it's one of my favorite things to drink. I'd only had water for so long, that it's a sweet treat. The burst of flavor it leaves on your tongue and the sugar, it's like a glass full of sunshine.

"Hello," I greet as I enter the room. Beau told me to always announce my presence. Where the Master wanted my silence, Beau and his father want the opposite. He says it's because being a cop and being involved with the Mafiya, they want to know who's around and who's listening at all times. I wouldn't dream of eavesdropping on them; they've shown me far too much kindness to do that to them. The Master was different. He acted as if I didn't exist the majority of the time and wasn't concerned if I heard him. I guess he always expected to kill me one day so it never crossed his mind if I heard them talk about business. I wonder if he regrets it now?

I shudder with the internal thoughts.

"You cold?" Beau asks, his gaze concerned while the other two men greet me in return.

I take the space next to him, on the other side a chair between them is his cousin and then another chair between them as well is his father. Spaced out like this, it's easy to see everyone as they speak. My lips turn up in a brief smile as I shake my head. The temperature's perfect. I was thinking of the monster that haunts my dreams and past.

I must've interrupted, as Viktor picks up on the conversation they were having when I came in.

"Help yourself, young lady." The older Victor nods to the spread and my eyes widen, trying to figure out what delicious item I should start with. I go for the orange juice as Viktor speaks to Beau and his father.

"So they told you that Russia is the next event. Did you find out if they're going to be out of the country more, or is this a special occasion?"

"This is definitely special. They invited me along, not only for the next auction but so I could be around to have my first pick as the women come in. I guess this is also a working trip for them to replenish the hoard."

I watch Beau aptly as he speaks, no amount of orange juice can wet my throat with the words he's just spoken. It's dry as I think what he means. The Master is going back to my beloved country to capture more girls and women. And the worst part is they want Beau to go too.

There's a good chance he'll leave and never return. Lots of men would show up at the Master's for special trips, and I'd never see them again. Not that I cared at the time about any of them, but this is different.

He places his favorite Russian pastry on my plate, offering me a smile as he continues.

"I think it's time to bring Finn back and have him go as well. I have a feeling this could be it, the perfect time to free them along with finding out where he has the others. With the right amount of money and trust, their lips will continue to loosen."

"I'll go too." Viktor nods.

"I don't know if that's a good idea."

"You need help, Beau. Let your cousins come. They know how to handle this sort and no one will cross you with the Mafiya and Bratva flanking you. And then you will be home, you will have enough men there and with you to shut these Sicilians down." Part of me wonders if this has been his father's plan, to have Beau get in deeper with the family business. He's eating it up that Beau isn't at home being a cop and everyone can see it.

"We're certain it's the Sicilians?" Viktor asks, taking a drink from his coffee cup.

"Don Franchetti." The older Victor nods,."Time to snuff him out. I should've taken care of it long ago. Back then he wasn't much of a threat, neither was his brother. Most of the other families stayed out of mine and Gizya's way. They all knew not to go against us."

"I can handle Bratva business," the younger replies tensely and I'm just sitting here flabbergasted that they're speaking like this in front of me. It's all so open and a little unnerving.

"Good?" Beau smiles kindly down at me as I pick at the powdery delicacy. He's no doubt already eaten several of them. I don't know how he can eat so many of the sweets and not get sick from it.

I nod, no longer smiling. I can't fake that right now, when I know the danger he'll be facing soon. Russia is a long trip too. That means they'll probably have to leave on Thursday. I remember when they first took me and they said we were leaving the country. It felt like we were on the plane forever; no way was it only one day to travel.

"I'll bring along Spartak and Alexei along with a few others. I'll see if Tatkiv is free and can bring some of his men as well. We need to appear like we're interested in buying."

"Leave Niko at home; this is too close for him," Beau responds, his attention back on the others. "I'm grateful for the men, but this trip has to be quick. I only have one more week off work before the chief expects me back. He has another assignment for me, and he's waiting."

That means he'll be gone even longer if he makes it back safely. How long would we be apart then? How long do missions or assignments or whatever last for undercover police officers? Is there a specific time frame? Two nights is bad enough; I can't imagine him being away for even longer. I need to be strong for him and I want to, but the depression eats at me when he's far from me.

"I agree, Niko needs to stay back. I'll tell my brother. We need to come up with a flight plan. Contact Capelloni, and make sure he won't spook if we show up."

"I will, I'll see what details I can squeeze out of him, pretending I'm over-excited for the new stock."

Beau's going to speak with Yema. I need to figure out a way to get him to take me with him.

"Who's Tory, by the way? I'd forgotten all about meeting him until I found his card in my pocket." Beau stares at his father curiously.

Victor grins, the first real smile about something that doesn't have to do with his own son. "Good ol' Tory. He is a field agent, FBI. I did not know he was still working."

"How do you know him?"

"He helped me a few times with problems. You do not need to worry, moy sin."

"No? Funny that right after I shake hands with the man, the FBI is calling the department to speak with me."

"He may want to know why you are there. He is good man, Beau. If you see him at these, use him, he can give you information."

Beau nods, but I can tell he's not completely sold on his father's information. I wait patiently, quietly biding my time until Beau and I can be alone, until I can state my case and get him to let me go with him. I have to protect him and I can help.

What you think, you become.

-Buddha

BEAU

"You can't make me stay here." Sasha glares while shaking her head and grumbling. I thought it was adorable when she began to plead her case to me about wanting to help me.

She was sorely mistaken, believing she could talk me into anything though. Our discussion went from polite and quiet to a full-blown screaming match in no time once she let it be known she was planning on coming with me no matter what I said. She's a stubborn woman that knows exactly how to push my buttons.

"I can and I will." I shrug.

"Russia's my home, I want to go."

"Nyet, your home's here now. End of discussion, let's talk about something else."

"You have to take me, Beau! This isn't fair," she declares angrily, not letting the topic drop. I'm a little surprised she didn't stomp her foot, with the determined look crossing her face. She's pissed and she's not letting me change the subject.

My hand shoots out, grasping a handful of her hair, pulling her close enough so she can feel my breath on her skin as I glower down at her, standing my ground and lay it out. It's for her protection. I hate having to try and scare her, but I want her here, in my father's house, safe. "I don't have to do shit. I saved your ass. Literally purchased you from your kidnapper's grip, and you're standing here, telling me that you want me to take you right back into the middle of that hell. Well, get over it. You're staying the fuck here."

"You're worse than he is!"

"Oh really? I don't recall stealing you away from your family and forcing you to have sex with me!" I shouldn't say it, but it happens before I have a chance to take it back. I don't want to hurt her more than she's already been, but I have to be a bastard to protect her from the real monsters.

"He wasn't like that," she mutters, her eyes falling to the ground.

No way she said those words...surely I heard her wrong. Sasha can't worry about that filth. "I can't believe this shit. You have Stockholm Syndrome."

196

"No, you're wrong."

"Am I?" Angrily, I palm her skull and shake her as I shout, "You mean to tell me, that you don't love him?" I've lost it. I'm too far gone for her, and even the thought that she could care for him has me going insane inside.

"Stop! Just stop it! You'll never find him," Tears fall over her cheeks and so help me, it makes me want to shake her harder. I want to make him completely disappear from her mind. Only one man should take up space there now, and that's me. I never should've gotten involved with her like this. I knew this would happen that she couldn't handle belonging to a man like me.

"Shut up," I growl.

"Without me you won't get to him." She sobs. "And if you do somehow figure out where he is, he'll never let you have the women, not without me there to help you."

Her declaration makes me sick inside. Dropping her hair as if she's a toxic virus, I step away. She needs to dispose him from her mind. He'll ruin her...he'll ruin us if he's still implanted in her thoughts all the time.

Another sob from her and she lets out a nearly-silent plea, "Please."

She no longer belongs to him. She's mine now, I've told her this, yet she wants to go back into the lion's den.

"Nyet." I state firmly. Twisting on my heels, I storm out of her room, slamming the door behind me.

"Let me out of here! I'm coming!" She screams through the barrier, pounding her petite fists against the wood.

Angry and hurt, I repeat myself. It's far too low for her to overhear me, but I have to say it. Not just for her, but for myself. "Nyet." I want to shower her with everything she could possibly wish for, but I refuse to give her this; her safety and life means way too much to me.

Sasha

Pounding until my hands ache and burn, my body eventually falls to the floor while I weep with sorrow. How could he treat me like this? He told me that I could say whatever I wanted and now that I have something to speak about, something to wish for, he refuses me. He's filled me with so much hope inside, so much love and now he's going to leave...again.

Each time is another chance he may not return. I've had the only person I cared about in my life stolen from my very grasp, and now it could be happening all over again.

All those women—stolen, raped, drugged, beaten, tortured, starved, burned to death, and he won't let me help him find them. I actually want to do my part. I'm okay here, being taken care of; I want to give them some peace too. For so many years I was unable to do anything or else risk my own death.

I have an opportunity to possibly save some of the others, but instead, I'm being forced to stay here, locked up in this room. It's like I'm a prisoner all over again, only Beau doesn't treat me like I'm worth anything money wise. He acts as if he can't touch me intimately like I'll burn him or something. Why can't he realize that I want this, I want to be with him?

Even the men who liked nothing more than to hurt me, offering up huge sums of money to have their turn, looked at me as if I were made of gold. The Master never let them buy me, biding his time, breaking me down piece by piece. Here I'm just a burden, the next charity case that's nothing but trash. I'm nothing compared to Beau and his father, even his cousin. Always trapped in a man's world where they believe they rule over everything. In my case, they do.

I have to figure out how to do something. There must be a way that I can help free the women caught up in this horrendous sex and drug trade. I'm not Nikoli's sister; I'm not someone they can control. I've been ordered around nearly my entire life, always having to please someone else. I know what the other victims are going through, what's expected.

Beau and his cousins have no clue. The type of men and even women that come to the auctions aren't people, they're evil. Beau is harsh, but he's nothing like the men I've come across in the past. He's not malicious.

Climbing to my feet, I head back to the window. I know it's secured by some high-tech lock, butI pull and push, trying to get the window sill to move even an inch. If I can just get it loose, maybe I can wedge something in between it to get it open.

I'm exhausted and the crying's draining away what little energy I have. I slept well last night, but not the nights before. The nightmares, hell, even just the shadows I see at night keep me scrambling, thinking it's one of the Master's thugs ready to grab me and haul me back to serve them. I haven't shared that with Beau yet. He thinks I'm afraid to be alone, but he doesn't know it's the nightmares that continue to haunt me that are so frightening.

I don't want to even think of that name or those men. They're the stuff bad dreams are made of, no doubt. The Master treats you like you're his pet at first. Which is fine when he feels friendly, but when he's angry, he beats you until you feel like an abused dog, scurrying into a corner, attempting to hide.

I shudder, remembering the shock of his fist hitting me when I was merely a girl.

There's a knock on my door, stalling my efforts of wrenching the window open to make my escape.

"Dear?" It's the maid. Beau's father's a very rich man. It's disturbing how wealthy men have no issues with locking women up in rooms in their mansions. And Beau—he's supposed to be different. No, he is different. He told me he

200

doesn't live like this, that he's normal. Yet, he didn't think twice about locking me away and demanding I stay put.

That's not fair. I shouldn't think of him that way; he's shown me so much kindness since I've been brought here. I can't help it though, I'm angry, the first real thing I want to do in my life and I'm being refused. Is it childish, my temper? Yes, but I've never been allowed to have one before and this is the first way that comes to me to express that feeling.

"Miss Sasha?" she calls again. She's nice and I'm ignoring her. The only person besides Beau who's tried to speak to me since I've arrived and I haven't given her a chance.

"Y-yes?" I reply. It's broken from my raw throat. I yelled as loud as I could through the door, but it didn't matter. Nothing sways Beau once his mind's made up, that much he made clear. He's normally so soft and sweet with me, but this time it was like facing a boulder that wouldn't budge, not even an inch.

"Are you hungry, dear? I have your supper."

"No. Please tell them I'm not eating," I reply stubbornly. It didn't work before, but maybe it will this time. The only other times I've gotten away with not eating is when he's gone away for the weekends to the auctions. As soon as he returns, he's lecturing me and stuffing me full of food.

"Please, Miss Sasha. You'll only make them angry, and you'll get weak from not eating. Let me bring this in to you."

"No. I mean it. I'm not eating until they let me out. He wants to be a boulder; I will be too." I didn't mean to admit that last part, but who cares, too late now. She probably couldn't hear me like this anyway.

"Very well then." I can hear the genuine concern in her voice, and as much as I want to eat, I'm too upset to. It's hard to eat when your body's wound up. You'd think I would've learned over the years to eat when commanded, and I did for the Master, but here it's the only bargaining chip I have.

Mere moments pass before my door's flung open with a furious Beau storming in, his cousin Viktor hot on his heels. The movement makes me jump and suck in my surprised breath.

Facing the two of them like this has my stomach twisting with anxiety. I don't defy men. I was taught over and over it's not acceptable, but Beau encourages me to speak my opinions out loud. It still freaks me out though.

"You're not eating now?" he huffs, his hazel eyes ablaze, his body still strung tightly from our previous argument. He's beautiful, full of so much passion.

"No. You'll let me go, or I'll starve myself."

"Why must you make this so fucking hard? I give you a safe place with a comfortable bed and good food to eat, yet you fight me at every turn it seems. I rescue you from a money-starved psycho, yet you yell at me to let you return. I'm done being nice. You'll eat or I'll strap you to that bed and put a fucking IV in your arm."

I've never seen him like this. I haven't known him for long, a month now, but he's never spoken to me full of demands. This is the man he was warning me about, that I wouldn't know what to do with if I was really his. Somehow after all I've been through in the past, even that crawling up my spine, I'm not frightened of him. I know Beau won't really hurt me. I can push him and he'll fight back, but that's all. I'm not scared of him. I adore him — my *one*.

"You won't touch me!" I declare, backing toward the wall. I have nowhere to run, to hide. I could dart for the door, but he's much too big and powerful compared to me. His strength mixed with his cousin's is no match for mine if I were to try to escape and go on my own.

"Susan, bring me her dinner," he commands, and the maid dutifully brings in a tray full of wonderful smelling foods. Viktor stares at us both, not bothered in the slightest that his cousin is keeping me locked away. He's a gorgeous man, but he's void of any emotions. He's scarier to me, because he clearly supports everything his cousin's doing, but doesn't show an ounce of emotion with any of it. At least Beau's calm until I push him; then he explodes and flies into an angry outburst.

"I'll spit it all out," I warn. It's juvenile, but that's what he's reduced me too. He's treating me as if I'm a child, so I'm acting like one in return.

His stern gaze meets mine, his irises ordering me to submit, but after giving in my entire life, I refuse to anymore. "You're testing my generosity."

"I don't want it. Keep your charity."

"That's it!" he shouts. "Vik, grab her and hold her arms."

"No!" I scream scampering back into the corner of the room. My arms and legs fly, attempting to ward him off, but it's no use. I have no idea what I'm doing. I've never fought anyone off me before. I was never permitted too. I simply had to obey them, whoever it was at the time.

Viktor easily hauls me up, holding my arms tightly and turns me so I face Beau. He towers over me like a tall building—strong and imposing—dwarfing me.

"Get off me! Let me go!" I yell, tears already running down my face even though I don't feel like I'm crying. That's how much my adrenaline spiked during our little scuffle. My heart's pumping so fast, it feels like it may fly out of my chest, yet my body's absolutely exhausted. At this rate, it's simply my mind still holding on, helping me fight. I should've eaten this last weekend while he was away. Maybe then I'd be a better match.

The sweet Beau I first encountered is gone. In his place is an angry man, pushed past his limit, stressed and ready to get his way. His arm shoots into my hair, ripping my head back, his hot breath panting over my cheeks as his chest heaves. "You will fucking eat. So help me. I didn't risk my fucking life to save yours for you to act like an obnoxious brat!"

I open my mouth to argue that he didn't come to save me or anyone else, but Nikoli's sister. I don't get a word out as he stuffs a chunk of bread in my mouth, holding his hand over my lips so I can't spit it out.

"Chew it," he demands lowly as tears leak from my eyes. "I'll keep you like this all night long if I have to. You can chew your food, or I'll drug you and have Susan feed you with a tube. Which do you want?"

He wasn't lying, saying the Mafiya blood ran through his veins; he does have it in him. Beau could be a very powerful man in the underground if he ever decided to take control of things.

Chewing the lump of dough enough to swallow, more tears fall from my eyes.

At this moment I absolutely cannot stand him. I hate my savior in the same sense that I've grown to love him, and that feeling makes me even angrier inside at him.

His breathing slows down the more I chew, the rage in his eyes dimming as he watches me. After I swallow half of it, he moves his hand away, peering down at me. I'm so furious inside, I can't help myself. He's beautiful, but I'm oh-so-fucking broken. Using the remainder of the food I'm chewing, I spit it out, all over his face.

The room grows silent, only filled with heaving breaths from all of us.

Beau doesn't even speak. His hands become tight fists and I slam my eyes closed, waiting for the blow that's sure to follow. The Master never would've stood for such behavior from one of his pets. I'd seen a girl do it before to one of the guards—Nick. That's where the idea to spit at Beau came from. The Master had Nick beat her to death in front of us as a lesson on misbehavior. Now I can only expect the same in return.

Will Beau do it or will his cold cousin be the one to finish me off?

Viktor's hands release me, and I'm trembling so badly I can feel myself shake. At the sound of the door slamming, my eyes fly back open. I can't help my curiosity to see if it was only the maid leaving or if it was Viktor as well. However, there's no one there. I'm completely alone.

Beau has even abandoned me after my outrageous behavior. He was so harsh with me though. I'm meant to be free now, yet he's forcing me to eat, forcing me to stay in this house.

This isn't freedom; this is a new locked cage with a new master, and I'm merely his little dove, left to sit inside.

Falling to my feet, I'm all cried out. I'm so upset the shakes won't stop and I can no longer cry. There's nothing to cry over, because I know I'm already dead—it's just a matter of time. This is the Mafiya, and they won't put up with someone like me, causing problems and disrespecting them.

BEAU

Furious isn't a strong enough word to describe how livid Sasha's made me. Hasn't she looked in the mirror? She's been damn near starved to death, yet she refuses to eat. Her frail little body is so malnourished, I was afraid Viktor was going to break her when she started swinging at him.

We had the doctor pump her full of vitamins and vaccines when he first saw her, but if she refuses a nutritious diet, she'll end up killing herself. No one will have to torture her or sexually abuse her; she'll put her own body through misery.

Stubborn woman.

Seeing her like that had me on edge, but at the same time, I'm so damn proud that she's found her fire inside. She's learning to fight back — to shout and cry, to argue and throw things. She's come far and it's only been a month's time. If she ends up gaining anything from her time here, it'll be that she's not afraid to speak up for herself.

Sasha's full of so much passion and strength, if only she could see it herself. After everything she's been through, she's got one hell of a fight swirling through her, ready to burst free. She's so fucking resilient if only she'd let me help her.

She'll never be strong enough to go anywhere if she doesn't start listening to me. And her thinking I'd take her to Russia. Not a chance while she's in this condition and *he's* still running loose.

I'll take Sasha to visit one day if she wants, but only after the leader of this sex organization has been caught and put to an end, along with any of his contributors. I want them all and I want them dead. There's no amount of sentence the justice system can offer that would match the heinous crimes these fuckers have committed against women. The only type of justice I can see fitting is killing them all and offering women out there a sense of peace, even if they aren't aware of it.

I'm shocked at myself right now with how I just treated her. I physically stuffed her mouth full of food. She had me so wound up though. She was shouting at me and demanding I let her go along, straight into the danger. There's no way I'm allowing that to happen. I want her as far away from it all as possible.

I never should've let her hear our conversation this morning at brunch. I wanted her to at the time in case she had anything to add to it. I wasn't expecting this to come from it though.

I've never struck a woman before, not even undercover when I've been around some really nasty ones. I had a chick stab me and pull a gun on me, yet I refrained from hitting her then. Sasha was another thing entirely. I wanted to wring her neck to get her to listen to me. I'm not the controlling type to tell a woman how to live her life. I'm not attempting to be her father, but this was infuriating. Just once I want her to listen to me and just fucking obey.

It's for her safety and well-being, nothing else. That's a lie; it's for my own peace of mind as well. I can't stand the thought of losing her after merely finding her.

My cousins' wives aren't in this life and my mother was pushed from it as well. It's all about safety and protecting those we care about. This life…it seems to be becoming more and more my own way of life as well.

One more week left, and I don't know if I can go back to being a cop. I think I may have sunken too deep this time to swim my way out like I have in the past. I've been undercover for months at a time, but this search for Niko's sister has plagued me for five fucking years. It's been like a cancer, taking over my body, piece by piece. It's consumed too much of me now.

I don't even want to return to bust some meaningless asshole. I want to devote my time to helping those that mean something to me. I've grown more selfish this past month, that's for sure.

When I look at myself in the mirror, I no longer see Officer Masters staring back at me. My reflection shows a tormented man seeking retribution, of a man ready to dole out punishment. Someone no longer standing behind the law, but ready to be his own judge, jury, and executioner of the guilty.

I'm corrupt.

Family isn't an important thing.

It's everything.

-Michael J. Fox

"I can't believe you just witnessed that" I grumble, meeting my cousin's amused gaze.

He shrugs, waving it off. "No big deal. Elaina was a bit temperamental when we first met as well. You can't lose control with them. Once they see what buttons to push, they open you up. That woman already has you wrapped around her finger, to be able to make you angry like that."

"I don't know what it is about her. Anyone else and I'm like a damn stone, but one wobble of her lip and I want to break someone in two."

He chuckles. "She has you hooked. I can see it. Rest assured, that feeling is normal when you find the right woman."

"She has me something, that's for sure," I agree taking a spot on the sofa in my father's sitting room. Sasha's in her designated bedroom, yelling and throwing stuff it sounded like when I locked the door to keep her put. She was way too pissed off, I wouldn't put it past her attempting to escape.

"She's stubborn, like my wife. You need to be careful. I learned the hard way with Elaina, and I was like you — ready to break someone in half."

"Don't I know it! She may have been under their thumb when I met her initially, but I was right about my first impression; she has a fire deep inside that small frame of hers."

"You're not letting her go with us, right? She would be an unnecessary distraction."

"Nyet. Definitely not. She'll get hurt, and I won't let that happen. I need to know she's safe, so I don't have to worry about her while we're handling things."

"About that. You realize it's not going to be handcuffing them and turning them over to a group of marshals or anything, right?"

"Of course, Vik. I know how things work in your world. I've been sucked into it for a long time now."

"I just don't want you questioning your morals and regretting anything. I understand if you want us to take care of them, so you're not involved. I respect your career choices, even if they're opposite from mine."

"I've come to terms with it; I don't think I can return to the force after this."

"What changed your mind? You've fought against your roots—against your father—for so long."

"The things I've seen, the undercover life, the sex organization now, and the search I've been on for five long fucking years has swayed me. I have the utmost respect for those upholding the law, but I can't do it anymore. I'm at my end. I've seen our justice system fail too many people on technicalities, some as simple as not having enough physical evidence, when we all knew they were guilty. Take Sasha for example, how long has this buying and selling of women been going on? I'll tell you—forever. And we're no closer to stopping it; in fact, the country's more worried about drugs and politics to take off their blinders to notice the real atrocities plaguing the world today. On the opposite side of the law, I can do things my way—put more bad men down for good—than if I had the law backing me up. They'd more than likely bust Finn, a guy not half as evil as the motherfuckers showing up to the auctions all because the others have more money. Finn's rich, but these guys rule the world. I'm done. I'm done letting them get away with it. Call me corrupt, call me damaged. Hell, call me a mercenary or the son of the former Bratva King. I no longer care, I want my own terms of justice."

He holds his hand out to me, and I shake it in return. "Well then cousin, welcome to the family business."

Part of me feels as if I'm signing my life away to the devil, while the other side feels like a burden has suddenly been lifted. I no longer have to do whatever I can to be the golden son, the complete opposite of my father. I'll never be him. I'll never be that type of evil. I'll continue to hunt down men with so much in common as him, but I damn sure won't be a fucking saint about it either. It feels so good to not have to fight against my nature, to not have to worry about not being good enough in everyone's eyes.

"Tatkiv will be pleased you're joining us. Will you stay out in California or move closer to family?"

"I'd like to be near you guys if you'll have me?"

"Of course, you're always welcome. What will you do with the little captive?" He nods toward the ceiling, meaning Sasha.

"I'll keep her," I reply honestly and an evil smirk overtakes his face. We're more alike than I'd originally believed, but that's fine, I respect my cousins a great deal. Family is everything in this life; it's only taken me a decent portion of my own life to come to terms with that fact. No more wasting time. I need to forgive my father. Not for his sake, for mine. I need to move my mother out here, no matter how stubborn she is. I know she misses Victor, she always has. And most of all, I need to live this other part of my life for me, no one else.

"With her so determined to assist us, we should leave sooner, before she has a chance to wiggle her way on board. Will Uncle have someone here to watch over her or should I send for some of my men to keep her in place?"

"I agree, and I'm not sure. I'll ask him. I need to put in a call to Finn too. I want him with us. When are we boarding?"

"First thing, it'll give O'Kassidy time to get here, or he can meet us in New York when the jet refuels if it's easier. I'll go home and get my men prepared for our trip."

"You're the only crime lord I know who rises early."

"You're surrounded by them, they're disguised as businessmen on Wall Street, and I'm no lord, I'm the King," he replies with a cocky smirk, reminding me of my father.

"I stand corrected." I grin and shake his hand as he leaves the room.

"Eight a.m.?" I call after him.

"Yep, just early enough to piss off my younger brother." He chuckles, and I hear the front door slam shut.

They're all damn crime lords to me, but if I'm going to be more involved on this side of the world, then I should keep in mind the correct terms. Viktor is 'King' and Tate is the 'Big Boss.' Nikoli, Alexei, and Spartak are their Generals. What would that make me? I'm certainly not a soldier for them. Do I need a label to feel like I fit in with them?

My father enters the room while I'm busily pondering my new title.

"If I'm not a soldier to my cousin's organizations, then what am I?"

215

He doesn't even blink, automatically replying. "You're family Beau; you sit at the top with them. No need to worry over a job description. This isn't your typical nine-to-five. It's the family business and you'll always have a place amongst them. Does this mean you've decided to give up California and your other life?"

"As much as I know it'll break your heart, me not being a police officer and all, yes, I'm changing careers." It's said with complete sarcasm. He's always wanted me to take his place, but that'll never happen.

Viktor fills those shoes, and I'm not as jaded as to deal in weapons distribution or anything else they have their hands in. I'll continue to help them search, and I'll shut down whoever I can find involved with the sex slavery.

I'm counting on my father to keep his word to relinquish my trust fund. He promised me if I ever needed anything, he'd help, but for my trust, he's always wanted me to be involved with the family. When I'm not busy, I'll help my cousins with their various businesses. They practically own half of Tennessee. I'm sure they can use me somewhere that doesn't involve breaking the law too badly. I'm not completely turned, after all.

"Do not confuse me with not being proud of you, sin." He's always called me son in Russian. "I may not have embraced your cop career, but I have always been proud of you since the day you were born. Even more so with the man you are now."

216

"Spaseeba." I nod and leave the room.

I can't handle when he gets like that, like a father should be. He's not always been this way. Our relationship has mostly been full of tension or else nonexistent. He's doing this whole new man, new outlook. I hope he's truly trying to change and this isn't his newest scheme.

I don't hear screaming anymore, not that I would down here, but I wonder if Sasha's calmed down yet. I shoot a text to Finn O'Kassidy and let him know it's time to play ball, and he needs to come here or else meet us in New York. After making myself a quick sandwich, I head to my room to pack. It's been a long day and it's damn sure going to be a long week. I need undisturbed sleep to be ready for whatever's coming my way.

Sasha

The sound from my door unlocking has my stomach twisting. Last night I didn't get to sleep next to Beau, and even through my anger toward him, I missed him. I've been thinking all morning about what to say myself and about what he'll say about our argument.

I'm sure he'll apologize, and we can make amends. He's never been unkind to me in the past, and I pushed him too far. I'm new to these discussions, and I have to learn the best way to get my feelings across to him without either of us exploding like yesterday.

I'm sure he was also upset that I was fighting with him while his family was visiting. I should've waited until we were alone in bed to bring it up after he'd been able to relax.

Susan pushes the door open with a timid smile. She's probably scared after seeing me throw my fists toward Viktor yesterday, but she has nothing to worry about. I owe them all an apology for how I treated everyone. They've done nothing but show me kindness. I am disappointed, however, that Beau isn't here to greet me first thing. I was really hoping we could talk before our day got started. I was looking forward to feeling him against me.

"Morning, dear. Sleep well?"

"Hi Susan, about yesterday; I'm so sorry."

"Shh-shh." She waves her hand. "No need for that, it's all right."

"I was very rude, and you've done nothing to deserve it."

"You were passionate; there's nothing to forgive. It's good you spoke up."

"Thank you." I return her smile.

"Are you hungry? There are fresh cooked waffles and blueberries waiting downstairs."

"Actually, I was hoping to see Beau first." I climb to my feet, easing my way toward the door. "Is he in his room still?"

Her smile falls and worry overtakes her gaze. "No ma'am, he's not."

"Okay, then I'll join him downstairs."

She doesn't reply, just follows along as I go from room to room on the main level seeking him out. Finally I come to the last room he'd be in, the sitting room. The only person there waiting is his father.

"Susan, where is Beau? Did he go for a walk without me?"

She shakes her head, meeting Victor's stern gaze.

"Did he have to leave somewhere?" I pry.

"Indeed, he did." Her eyes never waver from her boss's. I can tell she's being careful with what she says.

"Can you tell me where?" I press further, and Victor comes closer.

"My dear, how about you join me for breakfast, and we'll speak about moy sin."

"Okay, I was hoping to eat with Beau though, especially after yesterday."

"He had some business to attend to, so I'll have to be your breakfast date this morning."

The massive grandfather clock we pass on the way chimes nine o'clock, so wherever he had to go, he must've left early.

We each get seated, our plates piled high with waffles, fruit, butter, and syrup. I feel like I can't wait a minute longer to ask my next question.

"Do you know what time he'll return?"

His father chews his bite, swallows, and then meets my anxious eyes. "No, I'm afraid I do not."

"But it's today, right?" I've grown bold with my questions and my voice over the past few weeks. Before, I never would've dreamed speaking this way, or how I had yesterday, especially to a man like Victor.

"I make you a deal," he suggests with his thick Russian accent more prominent. "You take bite and for each bite, I answer a question."

I nod, taking a decent-sized bite, chewing it quickly and swallowing so he'll give in and tell me already.

"Nyet."

"No?"

"He will not return today."

The bite I just swallowed feels remarkably heavy, and if it were still in my throat, I don't think I'd be able to get it down all the way.

"I see." I sip my from my glass of chilled orange juice and think carefully over my next few questions. I've discovered with these men you have to ask the right thing—the right way—to get the information you want. "Do you know what day he'll return?"

He nods to my plate, and I choke down another small bite. It all tasted wonderful until I discovered Beau wasn't coming back today. Now my mind's racing where he could be and what he's doing. I wish he'd start taking me with him.

"He should return on Sunday."

So long!

"But that's nearly a week away! Did he go to Russia for the next auction? When did he leave?" Questions tumble free as my mind runs wild.

I can't believe he left without saying goodbye. Did I anger him that much that he just slid off into the early morning without mentioning it? It hurts knowing he left the way he did.

Victor stubbornly nods to my plate again, and so help me, I have to fist my hands as not to toss it. Taking a deep breath, I shove another bite in my mouth, not chewing so ladylike anymore, just trying to get it into my stomach, so the man will speak. The food's tasteless to me now as I swallow it down.

"They left the country, and moy sin wants you to stay here. I can keep you safe for him."

Why do I feel like I want to explode inside? He should've let me go with him. I know how to stay out of the way and I could've helped. It's infuriating. I need to come up with a plan to get out of here. How, I have no idea. I've never escaped from anywhere before. I've always been too frightened to attempt it. I saw what happened to those that did, and it wasn't pretty. It usually ended in a lot of blood from a sick hunting game involving the Master's dogs or the scent of burning flesh.

I know they wouldn't do that to me here though. Well, I know Beau wouldn't. He's more protective rather than controlling. His father, however, I'm not so sure what lengths he'd go to, to keep me secure. He's a lot harder inside than his son.

"Moy sin left a phone for you to call him on. He may not answer right away, but he'll return your call as soon as he has a quiet moment to do so." He pulls the small black device free from the inside of his suit and sets it beside me.

I stare at it. I have no idea how to use it. I've seen people use them, but I've never been allowed to. It has a shiny flat surface, and the rest is solid black plastic and metal.

He notices my expression, his brows furrowing. "These can be tricky young lady, let me teach you how to work this new model. Phone companies are always changing them up." He's smart and he's kind enough to word it so I don't seem like a complete fool and my heart softens toward him a bit. In another life, this man could've been family to me.

Family?

Like Beau would've married someone like me? How on earth could that thought even enter my mind. I haven't had silly thoughts like that since I was first stolen away and would dream I was waiting for a prince to come and save me. The prince never was there to marry me, only bring me safely back to my mother. It was the best thought my little head could conjure up at the time. I liked to pretend it was a game. The games helped get me through many years, pretending I was locked away in one of the useless fairy tales my mother would tell me about every night before I fell asleep.

God, I miss her. I can't help but wonder what my life would've been like growing up with her. She was so young and very beautiful. *No, I can't think of that now.* I know my system will go into shock enough not having Beau here helping me feel safe and cared for. I don't need to drag old thoughts in the mix as well.

I'm so stupid for believing Beau would see things through my eyes and let me help him. He's a man, and I'm in a man's world. I suppose I should be grateful he entertains my thoughts at all. I haven't had a man do that before.

I am grateful. But I have to figure out a way to leave. If I'm truly free, they'll let me go, and this'll be a test. Let Beau see if he likes me leaving without telling him.

Master used to taunt us and say, "While the Master's away, the mice will play." It was always a threat that he knew what went on at all times, even when he was away on a trip and we were left behind with the guards. I have an uncanny feeling the threat was toward everyone, not just us stolen girls.

In this case, Beau is away and I'm going to test the limits. See how much I mean to him and if I'm really free. I don't know where this sense of newfound bravery's coming from. Perhaps from them letting me have opinions and from the anger. It's been a long time since I've felt anger like this. I'd made peace with my life; it was over because I was simply theirs.

Beau flares something alive inside me though. He makes me practically manic inside but, in the same sense, makes me swoon. I actually care what I look like, what I sound like, what he sees when his gaze is on me. My emotions aren't shut off when I'm near him; they're on maximum overdrive.

Victor presses a button on the side of the device, making it light up and draws me from my internal thoughts.

"See you press this here to get it to come to life. There is no code. You swipe your finger across the screen, like this."

"My finger?"

"Da, the heat from fingertip will bring up the main screen."

I watch as his finger does indeed bring up a new screen with a mere swipe. It's bright and only has a few options.

"Hit this button with the picture of the phone." He pushes it and a few numbers pop up. "This is my cell, Beau's cell, Miss Susan, and then moy nephews Tatkiv and Viktor. You can call Susan if you cannot find her around here and need something. You call me if you need something and can't reach moy sin. If you are ever in trouble — in danger — you call moy nephews and tell them what is wrong with you."

"Why would I tell your nephews?"

"Because, moy dear, they will be able to help you, no matter what is happening."

"Like the auction?" I begin, and he nods.

"Exactly like that. Anyone takes you or gives you a rough time, and they will send some men to help you immediately. You belong to moy sin now; his family is the Russkaya Mafiya and the Bratva. You know what that means, Sasha?"

He never says my name, so I sense the seriousness in his question. "I believe so."

"It means he is powerful man."

I knew it once he told me about his cousins, but Victor is hitting it home. Beau is much more of a force than I'd suspected and from the little bits I've heard from his father, Beau could be the head of the Bratva had he not become a police officer and shed his family name to stay away from everything.

He said I belong to Beau, but Beau has made it clear that he doesn't own me, nor does he want to. I was right thinking his father is accustomed to a different life when it comes to owning a woman. Did he own Beau's mother? I can't help the question breaking free with my thoughts twirling around in my mind. He has me overfilled with questions and curiosity.

"Did you own Beau's mother?"

He sits back in his chair, his eyes a bit wider, shedding the ever present, ever sturdy mask that's always shuttered across his gaze. He's so unshakable, so unchangeable at all times, that his surprise has my stomach twisting.

"Nyet. We were arranged to be married as was custom. But that is in the past; we are no more."

He doesn't admit that he's never not owned a woman, though—just that it wasn't Beau's mother. I wonder what happened to them? Beau hasn't told me much, just that he's always been close with his mother and she wasn't in the same life as his father. I was confused at first, but now I'm suspecting that his father loved her enough to let her go too. Even if it was an arrangement, you can't help who you fall for.

Beau met me one weekend, purchased me another and here I am, hopelessly waiting around, praying that he'll keep me. Could he be like his father after all? Could he care for me and want to let me go because of it?

I wish I knew more about him, to know for sure. Regardless, I have to get away from here. If Beau doesn't listen to me, then I need to leave and try to come up with a way to help them find these other missing women.

"Thank you for the phone. May I be excused to try calling him?"

"I wish you'd eat more first, you need your strength. It is what he wants."

"Thank you, but I'm not hungry anymore. I want to hear his voice. I'm sure it'll make me feel better."

His eyes soften, and I've officially pulled off my first bit of deception. I've never been good at it before, but then no one's ever trusted me either. I was always under scrutiny if I spoke or moved around too much in front of the Master.

"Very well. Remember he may not answer, give him time, it's dangerous."

"Right. Thank you." I take the phone and head to my room. I'll need shoes for my escape...

Sapphire Knight

Success and rest don't sleep together.

-Russian Proverb

BEAU

We exit from the sleek, expensive town cars that were sent to collect us from the private airstrip. My cousins didn't go easy when it came to bringing men along. We're rolling ten deep and who knows how many they have set up waiting for us to pull this mission off. I didn't ask about those details, and they weren't discussed along the way. I trust them. We simply worried about sleeping so we'd be ready and alert for whatever once we finally touched down on Russian soil. This could be an ambush for all we know, and there's a chance we could be lacking sleep by the time we make it back to the plane.

Yema along with a group of men are waiting to greet us outside what appears to be a damn miniature castle, and as

229

one of them approaches me, two of our men step closer, standing in front of me like an unmovable wall. I feel what my father must've felt for the majority of his life — untouchable and dangerous. Those two are a wicked combination for a man to feel; it's empowering, and that's scary because it's also energizing and addicting.

"Welcome." Yema steps beside the soldier that approached first. "He's doing his job and checking for weapons, just following orders gentlemen."

I make my way between the two men shielding me. "I've never allowed you to touch me before and don't think I'll be allowing it now." I scowl and Yema grins. No doubt testing to see how far I'll let him push, but he'll learn that it won't be far.

To say I'm strapped, that we're prepared, is an understatement. I can feel the double shoulder holster hugging my favorite weapons against each side of my ribs. I have another Glock at my back and a smaller-sized gun strapped to my calf. I have a switchblade resting securely in the inside jacket pocket, two blades strapped to each forearm under my shirt and a razor taped to my ankle just in case shit goes south. I trained with SWAT and in hand-to-hand as well. I like to think I know how to hold my own.

I've been undercover for a long time, and they don't want to fuck with me when it comes to carrying. I've had to watch my back for far too long. I know Finn, Viktor, and Tatkiv are loaded down as well as the other men that came along with us.

I faxed in my resignation to the force this morning before I left my father's house. I knew there was a sizeable chance I'd be breaking countless laws on this trip and the Chief doesn't deserve it. He's been good to me, and in a sense, I feel guilty for quitting. I know he's been waiting for me to return—for things to go back to how they were—but I can't do it. There's too much unfinished business I need to take care of, and I don't think Sasha would fit in well if I went back undercover. She needs someone around all the time, not a man who can disappear for months at a time without any communication. She'd break more, and I'd never forgive myself. I'm planning on keeping her after this is over if she'll have me, and I need to get my ducks in a row.

Yema flashes a shark-like smile toward my cousins, trying to appear as if he's not intimidated, but he's probably shitting a brick inside. I told him I was bringing them, but I don't think he believed me. I also left out that Finn would be along as well. So many men with so many ties in one place, I wouldn't be surprised if we flagged Homeland Security with this little meeting. Hopefully, we were able to go undetected by any government agencies in case I put a bullet in these people's heads—my family and friend not included.

"Yema, this is Viktor Masterson, Tatkiv Masterson, and you remember my friend, Finn."

"Yes, yes...so nice to...meet you all." He glances at each face, clearly not sincere in the slightest. He's a snake, and we all know it. We just have to wait for the perfect time to chop off his head. "Sasha couldn't come along? Did you grow tired of the useless cunt already?"

I have to grit my teeth not to bite his nose off from him calling her useless. If anyone deserves that description, it's him.

"I gave her to my father." I shrug as if she was boring. Never mind the truth — that I fucking adore her and her fiery spirit and I want to cut this man in two.

"Good, we have plenty others."

"Here?" Finn inserts himself in the conversation, most likely sensing the hostility coming from me in waves toward Yema Capelloni.

"Yes, freshly picked this past weekend. If you're wanting them broken in, you can select them, and we can get them to you at a later time."

It's all so very professional. I roll my eyes. It makes me sick to hear him speak so flippantly about the lives of women. Good people, like Sasha no doubt, stolen away from their families and homes to be sold like cattle.

Viktor clicks his tongue in annoyance. "Who do I speak to about large purchases and when can I see the product? My men deserve some compensation."

Yema's gaze trains on my cousin, hearing his cold voice for the first time since we've arrived. Tate remains quiet as well — watching, waiting, and biding his time.

"I can help you with them," he replies, and Viktor snorts.

"I don't need help with anything. Fetch me your boss; I plan to spend a lot of money, and I don't speak to underlings."

I damn near choke with laughter. The men stand solemn, but I see amusement dancing in Finn and Tate's eyes at Viktor's choice of words. He just put Yema in his place with one sentence. No beating around the bush and this is only one reason why Viktor runs the Bratva so effortlessly. All those years he worked to be squeaky clean, and the trouble he went through with his father has made him grow a spine like steel.

"Come inside for a drink, and I'll get the Don for you." Yema nods, knowing Vik has him pegged for what he really is. Leave it to my cousin to make a man feel two inches tall with one sentence.

We still haven't found out who this infamous 'Don' is. My father has suspicions it's the Franchetti family running everything—old Sicilian wealth and roots embedded in the sex smuggling business throughout the years. After being so deep in it himself, I have a feeling he's most likely right. He's an ass, but he's a smart one when it comes to his business ventures.

One of Viktor's Generals wanted to come along just in case it was them. He has a hard-on for one of the Franchetti daughters and the last place he caught a glimpse of her was when he came to pick up the group of women I bought from the auction last week.

She took off before he could speak two words to her, but he's been pacing around like a caged animal ever since that night, according to my cousin. I'm afraid of what he'll do if he sees her here. It was already a huge shock for him to discover her involved in all of this. I think what little bit of a heart he had, left his body that night. Not surprising, this shit will harden you up fairly quickly.

I don't know the details of their story, and frankly, it's none of my business anyhow. I care about freeing these women, putting a stop to their business and hoping like hell to find Nikoli's sister somewhere along the lines. Five years and I'm finally making a touch of progress in this whole thing. A month of dealing with Yema is way too long for me.

We follow along, stepping inside the obscenely large home. It's bigger than my fathers. It reminds me of Tate and Viktor's father's place here in Russia. Gizya's estate is a massive compound with multiple buildings surrounding the main house. It could hold a large portion of Russia if it needed to.

I'm surprised to see the Sicilians have such a large estate here and that the Russkaya Mafiya would allow it. I wonder if Tate knew about this place or if he's already planning inside to have men overtake it. I wouldn't be surprised to see the men here cleared out, and the Mafiya claim it.

We're brought to an enormous room with multiple, plush leather seats, a buffet with a large selection of liquor, and a fireplace roaring with flames. It's chilly here, but the fireplace is large enough to ward off the coolness in the room.

"You may wait here while I alert the Don you've arrived. Mytroshka will get you refreshments." He nods to a young girl standing idly next to the buffet. Her gaze remains trained on the floor before her. He takes his leave, and the girl doesn't move an inch.

His men remain behind, standing in various places around the room, attempting to watch us without appearing so obvious. They do a terrible job at it, and we could easily overtake them if we needed to. It looks like they've been busy eating too much pasta to move quickly.

Finn approaches the girl. "Scotch, if you will, lass."

She never looks up at his face, turning quickly and efficiently to pour his drink. No doubt she's been 'trained.' After finding Nikoli's wife when she was kidnapped, in the terrible shape I had, it's been harder and harder to keep my mouth shut. I wonder how long this one's been here.

God, the shit they did to Sabrina was horrendous. I'll never forget how bad her lips had gotten—they were cracked and peeling, stuck together. I had to paint her up with Vaseline each day just to get her able to speak. The poor women went through hell.

It was amazing I was able to infiltrate their organization in the UK and eventually free her. Of course, there were casualties, but those pieces of shit deserved to die. It was so awful; I wanted to burn the entire place down.

Yema enters the room pulling me away from my dark memories, followed by four additional men. The one in the back is older, more distinguished; I'd say my father's age. He has a sprinkling of grey through his thick black hair and a natural tan from his heritage. Yema stops in front of us as we all come to our feet. He stares at the man as if he's a god.

"Gentleman, may I introduce the Don Franchetti."

The men flanking him carry forty-fives as if it's a goddamn soda or something. It's reckless, keeping your weapon drawn like that. It may be pointed at the ground for now, but it takes one person getting pissed off to raise it and shoot.

Our men notice as well and move in closer, ready to protect us if needed. This is the last thing I need to worry about. It's already dangerous without live weapons drawn.

Viktor steps forward, his hand out to greet another boss in the life. Granted they aren't Russian, but my cousins will be respectful until provoked. They'd expect the same if the roles were reversed. After their exchange, Tate follows and then me. The others remain silent, not needing to be a part of the conversation.

"I hope Yema has made you comfortable." His accent is thick, matching his looks. He stands out like a sore thumb in Russia; he belongs in Italy.

It infuriates me knowing he comes to the country I'm from to steal women and children to torture and sell. It angers me in general; but the fact he comes to my country to do it is like driving a knife under my finger nail.

"We're fine." Viktor nods. "Where are the women we were promised to pick through?"

Straight to the point—my cousin. I like it. The sooner we get done here the better. I want to get this over with and return to Sasha as soon as possible. I know she's called, but I haven't checked my phone. I've kept it on silent. Once I see her name on the screen, I'll be able to think of nothing else. All that matters right now is that she's safe, waiting for me and I'm one step closer to shutting this asshole down.

"I was under the impression you'd be staying with us for a visit."

"Whoever told you that was wrong. We came because we're interested in seeing your stock. Of course, we'd want to see how they're kept and if you have others available. Unfortunately, we're short on time. You understand, of course."

"You want me to show you my hand, in other words," Franchetti grumbles, glancing at Yema with irritation.

"We like to know exactly what we're investing in. We'll make you an even richer man if you work with us a little. If not, that's fine; we can head back to the jet and stop wasting your time. I'm sure it's precious as is mine."

The Don nods. I'm surprised he's giving in so easily, but I've been buying women from him for weeks now; hell, over a month. He has no reason to suspect me. And Viktor, well he's a straight shooter with one hell of a reputation following him. You don't get dubbed 'the Cleaner' in this business because you know how to spray a bottle of 409.

"I was hoping your father would have accompanied you." His gaze meets mine, and he confirms my father's claim to have known him.

Great, old buddy's reuniting. Not on my watch, pasta eater.

"He's overseeing a few things in the States." Like my woman, not that it's any of his business.

"Ah, a shame, he was always a reasonable man."

And this guy clearly lies through his teeth. There was nothing reasonable about my father when he was in the game. I'm sure Franchetti's just happy to have him out of the way so he can control the sex slavery industry. My father would've mowed him down had he gotten in his way back then. I've heard the horror stories. It's one of the many reasons why it's so difficult for me to have a relationship with him.

"My father's a hard man, we all know this." He nods, his lips turning up at the ends in nearly a smirk. I'm not going to bullshit him over common knowledge.

"I hear you've been enjoying some of our selection already."

"Then you hear right. I've kept one for myself; the others have gone to the men."

Spartak attempts to appear casual, but I see him scanning each corner and shadow every so often. I doubt Don Franchetti would have his daughter hiding in a corner or having her prance about where we can get to her easily.

"I was curious, is the announcer you have at the auctions available to purchase as well?" Spartak blanches hearing my question, but I'm sure he'll figure out I'm only asking for him.

The Don grows deathly still. All eyes fall on me as I test him. Will he admit she's his daughter or will he pass her off as some unattainable employee?

"I understand you two are married." He gestures to Viktor and Tate and then turns back to me. "But you are not?"

"No, I'm not."

"Perhaps we can discuss a merger of sorts if you're truly interested in that girl. Let's leave that for later after you've seen the product we have here."

No fucking way he means what I think he does. He can't expect me to marry his daughter, surely. I'm here to buy women or pretend too, and I just admitted I kept one for myself already. Is he not worried about his daughter marrying a monster?

He's worse of a man than I originally believed. I'm the enemy whether we come right out and admit the fact or not,

239

yet he's thinking of using his printyessa daughter to merge the families together. My Russian ancestors must be flipping over in their graves right now with this new turn of events. I'd never put much stock in who I'd end up marrying, but now that I've met Sasha it's a viable subject. Hell, would she even want to marry me eventually? Maybe someday. Clearly, I'm missing her right now to be thinking of this at the moment.

I can feel Spartak's gaze beating down on me from bringing Victoria Franchetti up, but he can relax. I'm not interested in her in the slightest. Surely he knows that I was merely asking for him and that I'd never marry her.

"Bring your drinks if you'd like, we'll go see the supply." The Don gestures, turning to leave the room.

I'm glad Sasha didn't come along. I don't want her anywhere near these people. I can't help but wonder if she would've been happy to see him and how she could care for someone like him. He's warped her into thinking she doesn't deserve freedom and that her purpose is to serve men's deranged needs. If she came with us and he were to touch her or speak to her, I'd lose it. I wouldn't be able to keep it together; it's hard enough now being in the same room and being close enough to kill him. Thinking back to her pleading to come with us has my blood boiling. I hope I get to put a bullet in his skull before we return home.

Franchetti and his men exit the room, and we follow along. We hold back just a bit, allowing them to lead us through hallways and down concrete steps until we come to a basement. We need to get the layout if there's any hope of rescuing these women.

There's a trickle of water echoing, coming from somewhere nearby, accompanied with an uncomfortable silence. Along each wall are concrete type cells that run the length of the room. They're tiny, and each cage has a gate made of fencing securely locked with a padlock.

I can't believe with how rich this man is and how big the estate is that they don't have a better security system in place. I guess he thinks the guards are enough. It's never good to be too cocky or complacent.

Some women gaze at us, their fingers tangled in the fence to keep them upright. They look weak and drained, probably from not being fed and from being tortured. Or as Franchetti and Yema would call it, being put through their 'training' to be sold at another auction. Just looking at them has me wrecked inside. How could someone do this to another human being? I'll never understand this type of thinking.

Other cells seem empty until we pass by the doorway and you can see the women huddled in corners. They're naked and absolutely filthy. I'm assuming the dark spots on the concrete around them are from old piss and bile.

Most of them shake; others have silent tears trailing down their faces. It's too much. I feel like I'm going to explode. My fingertips dig into my palms; the short, trimmed nails are blunt, but my grip's so harsh I can feel them dig into the calloused flesh of my palm. It's taking everything inside me not to rip these men apart with my bare hands and save these traumatized women.

I can't though.

I have to hold my emotions back, beat them down into the cracks running through the floor beneath us. Holding my breath, I scowl, coming off as the annoyed rich boy. My heart is shredding, piece by piece weeping for each new face I find as we walk the perimeter. Somehow, someway, I will get them justice for this.

After a brief viewing of each woman, we head back up the stairs and end up in a library. I'm too irate; I can't even speak at the moment. I have no words available that will make any sense right now. I thought I knew rage before. I hadn't a clue what true rage was until a moment ago.

This time it's Tate that takes the lead; he's dealt with a lot of this. He's been cleaning up the Mafiya over the last six years, and he's come across women in this state several times. I know it affects him, but he's learned to wear his mask better than I have.

"So? Do we have a business deal? What are your thoughts on the selection?"

"They were fine. We'll take the evening to discuss it at our place and make you an offer first thing. They need to be cleaned up and fed though, preferably sooner than later. I won't take them on the plane in that state. They could die on the trip like that and what use would they be to my men if they're dead?"

The Don's eyebrow shoots up, not amused in the slightest with having to spend time or money on the women without knowing how much he'll make off them in return.

"And what guarantee do I have that you'll even offer a fair price for them?"

"None of this business is fair. I'll offer you an amount by wire transfer, and then you can give me the location of the next, assuming there are more. This place was too small for the number of women you've promised. I'll buy the others from you as well. How many facilities do you have in total?"

"You've seen everything; I would prefer if you stayed the evening here rather than a hotel."

It's not a request, and it'll change the original plans we had. We were supposed to scope everything out and get the location of the women. Also, a guard count and then tonight Tate's Mafiya guys would hit this place vigorously to take the women to safety and hopefully kill the Don. We were supposed to be on our way to the next location when this all went down. If we stay here, it won't go as planned. It's not like we have anywhere to discuss the change either. I want this man six feet under and soon.

"We're gracious of your hospitality, but we have family waiting for us. This is my country, and I have my personal estate." Tate stands taller, more imposing to lay it down we won't be kept here. He is the Big Boss in Russia, not the other way around.

"Of course, then perhaps a few of your men would like to stay to show good faith."

Tate and Viktor's jaws harden, knowing the danger they'd be inflicting on the men. Another aspect though, it may be good to have a few men inside. It will also be very unsafe for those men while we're not around.

"I'll stay," Spartak speaks up, and Viktor's stern gaze flies toward the man he trusts to protect his wife. She would be devastated if something happened to him and seeing her like that would rip Vik apart. I know it's because he wants the chance to hunt the estate for Victoria. He needs to watch his back, though, or he could end up getting himself killed.

"Boss." A few of Tate's men step beside Spar, volunteering as well. They're loyal soldiers, ready to sacrifice on a whim.

This really could work, having a few on the inside when the others hit tonight. We're all thinking it. We just need the locations of where the other women are so we can be on the way to save them as well.

"It's done." Tate gestures to the guys and Franchetti relaxes, pleased he got some leverage out of it.

"Where are the others?" I ask, finally getting my bearings.

"We'll get to that after the deal tomorrow," he responds, and my stomach sinks. We need the info now to go through with the plan tonight. *Fuck.*

"My fault," Viktor interrupts. "We need the flight plan now for where we'll be off to the next few days. My pilots need to know how far the flights are to call in additional if we need them. I take my safety seriously; I won't have some coked-up men half-ass fly me around the world. I'm sure you understand."

It's a challenge to the Don to see if he'll cave if he's confident enough to give us the places. It's a question of trust, and they have no reason not to trust us so far. Well, besides the fact that we're Russian and belong to different crime families.

"No harm in giving you the cities, I suppose." He goes to a side table scribbling something on a small piece of paper. When he's finished, he hands it to Viktor. My cousin glances over it and nods. I can tell it's not what he wanted, that he's not pleased.

"Thank you." Viktor shakes the older man's hand, and we all follow suit. Yema leads us to the door, and it's not until we're in the safety of a moving vehicle, heading for their vacation house, that Viktor lets loose a string of curses in Russian.

He's livid and already pulling his cell free to dole out orders and change up what we had believed was going to be a foolproof plan. I take my own phone out and notice one missed call from Sasha, but that's not what worries me...it's the ten missed calls from my father that has my heart pounding.

They tried to bury us.

They didn't know we were seeds.

-Mexican Proverb

"Sin?" My father answers on the first ring.

"Da."

"Thank you for calling."

"What's going on?"

"Have you spoken to the dove?"

"I tried calling her back, but she didn't answer."

He swears in Russian, clearly upset about Sasha. That's not good at all.

"I do not like worrying you when you have other things happening."

"Tell me what's going on, please."

"I gave her the phone as you wished and now she's gone. She stole the money Nancy had for groceries and slipped out. She took Bruno's car."

"Shit, she doesn't know how to drive. She doesn't know anything about the regular world. Fuck!"

"She knew enough to get away."

"How did she get past the gate in his car? Where was everyone anyhow? She's one tiny woman, and she walked right out the door?"

"She slipped out, and Bruno had his car parked outside the property. Keys in ignition, sure no one would bother it."

"Fuck. He's an idiot," I groan, as we pull up to my cousin's massive spread of a vacation home. "Have you found her yet?"

"Da. The phone was a good plan, sin. I've traced her to a small hotel only twenty miles away."

Twenty miles too far.

"Okay, send someone to watch her quietly, please. Leave her alone unless she tries to get any farther or if your man reports anything suspicious. I want to give her space until I return, if possible. As long as she's safe and no one bothers her, that's what I worry about."

"I could have my men snatch her up, and we can lock her back in the room? Then you don't have apprehension over her. This will not happen again, moy sin."

"Nyet. I appreciate it, but she has to learn to spread her wings. I'm here with Yema and Franchetti, so they shouldn't be thinking of her right now. Your suspicions were correct about Don Franchetti being in charge of this entire thing."

"Be careful Beau; he plays to win."

"Well, it's a good thing I'm not used to losing then."

"Da. Be safe, and I'll watch the dove for you."

"Spaseeba."

"'Tis nothing," he replies and hangs up.

Fuck, fuck, fuckity-fuck. Not good and the last thing that needs to be going on right now.

I really hate it that she's out and about with me being in another country. I need to be there to protect her, but by me helping snuff Franchetti out, I will be protecting her from far away. Still, she's like a newborn colt walking for the first time, and it has me full of anxiety. I don't want anyone to take advantage or hurt her.

Hopefully, this will make her stronger and show her it's not bad being a free woman. What would she do on her own and for the first time? I asked if she wanted to shop or eat anywhere and she wasn't interested. Could she have other ideas? I should've asked more questions, paid better attention to her when I was there.

"Everything okay, cousin?" Tate's brow wrinkles as he studies me putting my cell away.

I know Viktor's curious as well, but he won't ask. He keeps his nose out of stuff that doesn't directly involve him or the Bratva for the most part. Tate, on the other hand, is nosey and not at all afraid to butt in.

"It's Sasha; she's left my father's."

He laughs.

He fucking laughs while I'm twisting with worry.

"Typical woman, so stubborn. Give her time; she'll be back." He waves it off, clearly used to dealing with tenacious women.

"How can you be sure she won't leave for good? I wouldn't make her stay, but I want her to."

"We're Mastersons. We pick headstrong women, but in the end, they're loyal, just wait. She may put up a fight with you, but when you show up, she'll still be yours." He grins his cocky smile and pops a chocolate in his mouth from the dish on the entry table.

As much as I love Russia and the food, I'm not a fan of their chocolate. It's not as sweet as the states or say chocolate from the UK. Australia is another one that has good chocolate and caramel.

"Vodka?" Viktor offers, heading for the study and I follow. Now Vodka in Russia is a whole other thing. It's like a fine wine to Italians; it's dry and utterly delicious.

"Of course. So what are we doing about Don Franchetti and Capelloni?"

"He named three places on the slip of paper he gave me. Of course, they're merely names and no addresses."

"Figures," I grumble, and Tate huffs.

"One is Italy; the second is China and the last, Miami. I'm suspecting China because it's so overly populated it'd be easy to snatch women and then also the lure of the small women from there. Italy we can probably figure out. I'm assuming it's his home residence. Miami is close to the port to take in women from Cuba and then imports from Spain. The downfall is it's so general; these holding places could be anywhere in these three. We're going to have to offer him a wire transfer and wait to overtake each place as we figure out where they are unless he trusts us and gives up the location. I'm just worried he'll eventually send us on with Yema and he will go underground. Most likely his brother will disappear as well, and then we'd have the places but be fucked on taking out the leaders."

"It's turning into a shit storm. We'll have to keep Franchetti with us. Maybe say we won't buy unless he personally escorts us, like a deal without him there would be disrespectful?"

"It could help sway him." Tate nods. "But who's to say he'll bring more women back to these areas? We need to get the women out and have each location watched and ready for a takeover."

"It's a lot of men." Viktor taps his finger along the bar thinking, then pours three tall glasses of vodka. If I hadn't gotten accustomed to more Vodka lately, I'd be on the path to blitzed with this amount of liquor. When I was undercover, I drank but limited myself to a few shots. It was always smart to keep my wits about me.

"Aw, bro, we can pull it off." Tate takes the glass from him, tipping it slightly in a salute before downing a large gulp. Their fathers always drank like a fish and started Tate and Vik on it when they were eleven. Thankfully they can pace themselves and haven't let the alcohol ruin their lives. I'd be surprised if they don't need a new liver at some point though.

Viktor holds the glass to me.

"Spaseeba," I acknowledge before taking my own drink. It's good—chilled and crisp—just the way fine vodka should be.

"We'll figure it out. I propose we offer one point five million for the group he has here."

"No way, he'll never go for it. I say we start at five million," Tate counters.

"The auctions I've been to the women go for a few hundred thousand each easily, and that's only one woman at a time."

"Right, but we're proposing to buy him out this week in three locations. Fine. Twenty million, with payout at the end of the week when all sales are final."

"You're going to try to get the women and take him out before transferring the money?"

"Of course. He thinks we're fools. We play this patiently like the past month, and we'll come out on top with what we want and keep our money."

Tate snickers and I smirk. His plan is good, and with the relationship I've already built, it could happen.

"Let's do it."

"Hell yeah."

"Good, I'll call my men and get them into place. Tatkiv, I trust you'll organize your men, and Beau, keep up the charade. I can see that they buy everything you feed them and it's perfect."

We toast, clinking our glasses together lightly and down a good portion.

"What about Niko's saystraa? None of those women he has were tall like she would be."

Tate's fist hits the counter top. "Fuck, I don't know if we'll ever find her. It seems like crate after crate we find or each woman we come across and not an inch closer. I feel so terrible for moy brat."

Viktor nods, gazing into his drink. We have a lot on our plate, and Niko will be brokenhearted if we return without her.

"I need sleep," I admit, exhausted even with sleeping on the plane ride over.

"Me too," Tate agrees easily, throwing back the rest of his liquor before placing the empty glass on the bar and standing from the stool.

"I'm taking a nap," he announces, and I follow, standing up.

"Me too." Hopefully, my father has eyes on Sasha at this point as well.

"Good. I'll put in a call to my Printyessa and do the same." Vik nods to each of us, "Brat Beau."

"Brat," Tate replies to his brother and pats me on the shoulder.

"Viktor." I nod back, and we all head in our separate directions.

I try Sasha again before I go to sleep but get nowhere. I wasn't expecting her to answer, but that's fine. I'm just grateful she's not mindful of the tracking device her phone has, so I can keep tabs on her. One thing is for certain; I sure do miss her next to me in bed.

Sasha

Beau's called twice now, and I feel guilty for not answering. He's helped me, but my anger overshadows his kindness. He left me again, and this time didn't say a word about it. He could be killed, that's a very real scenario, and he shook me off as if I know nothing. I can't sit around and just wait when he is in danger like that. I should be with him, helping them with the Master and Yema.

Yema already didn't care for Beau; he thought he was just a stupid Russian, but not my Beau. He's smart and resourceful. If anyone can survive, it would be him; he's good at hiding. At least that's what I have to keep telling myself, so I don't freak out.

This is why I never became close with any of the other women and children that were kept captive with me. Not only were they competition for staying alive, but because what if I loved one, had an actual friend and then the Master had her sold off or killed? My heart was already too messed up to let anyone close or let any more pain inside.

I plop down on the uncomfortable bed in the hotel I found off the side of the road I was driving down. I can't believe I actually drove a car. It was terrifying and exciting all in the same breath. I was lucky to find a bigger road to turn onto a few miles down from Victor's mansion, and it led me to a motel.

The man at the front didn't ask for any form of identification; he just waited for me to hand over some cash and gave me a key that's hooked to a diamond shaped piece of old blue plastic. I parked the beat-up red car I'd taken on the side of the building, so hopefully, no one will find me; that's if they even look. I'm sure they'll want the car back, but I'm not so sure about me. Although Beau did say that he had to pay for me, even being sick and unresponsive in front of everyone. I don't remember any of it, as I was passed out. Thank God he was there, or I may have died. None of the others there would've cared; they would've just burned my body to make me disappear.

That thought has my insides spinning.

Ugh, those memories make me feel even guiltier for making him worry. Am I being a pest by leaving? I have to do this, for my sanity. If he hates me because of leaving, I will never be able to forgive myself. But he's a kind man; I think he'll forgive me. I hope so at least. His father, however, I'm a little frightened as to what he'll do if he's the one to find me.

I doubt I'll be able to sleep much either. I may be alone here but the walls are thin, and I can hear people yelling, arguing, and swearing about things.

It's always better having Beau beside me, his hands securing me to his sturdy body. I hope he's safe; I want to have him close and inside of me again. I've never felt such pleasure as I have with him. Other men were so careless and unpleasant, but Beau, he can make me pant with his fingers alone.

The first night we were together was surprising with the way he touched me. He made me feel like I was special to him and then there were the intense sensations he made my body feel all over—every crevice was singing in surrender. I'll never forget him for as long as I live. I couldn't, no matter how hard I tried to. And his beautiful eyes, those will be burned into me for forever—with the way he's gazed at me so tenderly.

If the Master kills him, I vow right here, right now, that I'll find a way to return his punishment. I'll figure out a way to bring the Master to his death if it's the last thing I do. I only hope it doesn't come to that.

Sapphire Knight

If you chase two rabbits,

You will not catch either one.

-Russian Proverb

BEAU

The past few days have been hell with all the traveling we've had to do. I can't believe it's not over with yet. First, it was Russia; I'd forgotten how much I love the country I came from. I want to bring Sasha to visit someday so she can see her home as well. I hope she returns to me. I still haven't heard from her, and it's driving me mad inside.

The second stop was Italy. I'd never felt so outnumbered before, even doing my undercover jobs being knee deep amongst criminals in the States. Don Franchetti could've easily had us all murdered had he wanted to, but alas, money is too important when there are high amounts of it involved. On the upside, the food was delicious, even if I was paranoid taking each bite of it.

Then we stopped to look over the supply of women they had in China. It truly was another country. It reminded me of New York on steroids — so many people and they were everywhere. I was completely jet-lagged by that point; everything was a blur. My stomach is churning from the array of foods. I'm eating Tums like they're mint candies trying to find some relief.

When we finally touch down in Miami, I could kiss the ground. It feels great to be back on American soil with the humidity hugging my skin in a warm greeting. The flights were long, stressful, and exhausting.

"Alexei, remember our conversation," Viktor orders the General as we come to a stop in front of a Spanish-style mansion. It's smaller than all the others we've visited so far but the cost of living here is much more expensive, so it's not surprising.

I was present for the conversation he's talking about. Someone has to stay with Don Franchetti at all times, and Alexei has to drop a sonar device somewhere that won't be noticed, so our men have the full layout details to get to the Don tonight when we overrun each property. The men are all waiting for our go to save the women and either kill or take the prisoner, the men working for the Don. Most likely they'll die. At this point, I have no sympathy for any of them. They lost the possibility of mercy being shown to them long ago.

I can't stop thinking about Sasha. I wish she'd speak to me, but the phone has done nothing but ring each time I try calling her. She's stubborn, even more so then myself I think. Even with all the drama happening on our end, she's never far from my thoughts. It's dangerous being distracted like this, but it is what it is.

"Everyone ready?" Tate asks, gazing at each of us, waiting for our nod before opening the door on the latest town car.

I know now, I'd never have been able to pull this entire operation off if it weren't for my two cousin's help along with their men. Not just because of their money, but also because of the backup they have behind them and the extra bit of strength they offer me that I hadn't realized I needed. Everything is so much easier in this life when you have people standing beside you. It makes me wonder if I'd been around them growing up, if I would've been in this life from the get-go, and if it would be me in Viktor's position right now.

I'm happy he has it; I just can't help but think that things would've been different for all of us.

Sasha

There's loud banging, rattling the door and when I peek through the tiny peephole, I'm met with a mammoth of a Sicilian. Part of me thinks my nightmares have just come true. They've come to collect me and bring me back to the Master. But how did they find me? I've been gone only a few days from Victor's home. Unless there have people watching me, or maybe Beau. They have men everywhere, I'm sure of it.

Another bang that shakes the thin wood door and I'm quickly turning to the phone, lighting it up and hitting Victor's number. He answers immediately thankfully.

"Da?"

"Sicilians." I choke out, my hands beginning to tremble. I don't want to go back there again. "What do I do? "

He's shouting at his men is fast Russian while listening to me. He has someone close by he says.

"You go to the bathroom and lock the door, quiet as a mouse. My men can be at your location in three minutes, barely enough time for them to break through both the main and bathroom doors."

I rush to the minuscule hole of a bathroom and lock the door. It's flimsy and cheap, so I wrap the plastic shower curtain around the handle and tie it to the towel rack. It may only help for seconds, but that could be just enough extra time for Victor to get here.

"Door locked?"

I whisper, "Da."

Is there a window?"

"Da." I shakily reply again.

"Look out it and tell me if anyone is there."

"Da, two."

"Good girl. Lie in the bathtub and don't move until you hear my men call you little Dove."

"Spaseeba," I speak the Russian words I've heard Beau say so many times. They bring me comfort.

He hangs up, and I can hear my heart thundering in my chest. It's been a long time since I was scared enough for the pounding in my ears to be so vivid.

The door to the hotel room bursts open with what I'm assuming is a curse in their language. My teeth begin to chatter next, and I may chip one if I can't get myself to calm down. It sounds as if they're tossing the mattress and the closet door bangs open. The small set of drawers that are screwed into the wall are all ripped out, and I swallow, my throat bone-dry as they tear the room to shreds.

"Stupid woman," I hear the pissed off man who was at the door grumble.

"Check the bathroom, she's here hiding; no one saw her leave."

The heavy steps draw near the room and then three loud sounding thuds. It's as if there were three of them and they suddenly fell to the floor or into a wall. It's silent afterward, no noise at all except my labored breaths.

I concentrate on breathing. I'd stopped when I heard them talking. A few beats pass then a sturdy but kind, "Little Dove? Are you hurt?" It's said with a Russian accent, not like the Sicilians.

Relief. Jesus, I feel relief like no other at his voice. It's Rolo, one of the guards from outside of Victor's home.

I stand, but my legs are a bit wobbly with adrenaline thrumming through my body at nearly being discovered by the bad men. I know Victor's guys aren't the greatest people either, but they've been kind to me.

Unwrapping the plastic curtain from the door, I open it a bit and peek my head out.

I'm met with Rolo's goofy smile. The same one he always gives me when he's smoking out in the garden and I go for my walks with Beau. It's comforting to see a familiar face.

"Come, Little Dove. Boss is not happy. "

I asked before why they all call me such a silly name. Beau says it's because I'm like a tiny bird who was caged but belongs free. He says I deserve to fly when I want to. Does this time count or will I be scolded?

Seeing him is reassuring, but not nearly as much as when Victor's solid frame enters. He steps over the now-dead Sicilians spread out on the floor like he's attempting not to get his expensive shoes dirty. Victor's older, but he's still strong like Beau and very handsome in his own way. I would guess when he was a younger man, he looked just like Beau.

He holds a hand out toward me, and I place my small palm in his. He's never touched me before, and I see it for what it is, a peace offering and to give me a sense of comfort. I'm grateful more than he can imagine.

"You're not mad?" I gaze into his stern eyes, mine full of caution. He has every right to be furious, to punish me. I know the Master wouldn't have shown me kindness. He most likely would've killed me as an example to the others for thinking about being free, maybe worse—torture of some kind.

"Nyet." He tugs me a bit closer to him, towing me toward the door. On our way outside, he gestures to my room, making a sweeping motion with his hands and his men go to work cleaning up the bodies and blood like it never even happened. An easy feat for them with their training to make it all disappear.

There's a shiny new, dark gray Cadillac SUV idling at the curb. It's a flawless vehicle and screams wealth. None of the shady people standing about outside and around the hotel glance our way. They all stare at the ground like one look at us will seal their fate, and with Victor, perhaps that fear is true.

Another guard climbs out of the driver's side and opens the door closest to us. Victor steps to the side so I can scramble into the back first, then he follows. The door closes quietly after him, and we're encased in silence and darkness from the nearly-black tint on the windows. The air's rich with a heady leather scent from the interior and his spicy aftershave.

"The men in the back!" I suddenly remember, and he shakes his head, raising his hand to calm me.

"They've been taken care of. No one will harm you," he responds with finality as we pull away from the cheap motel.

"Why aren't you angry?" My gaze is still wary as I twist my hands in my lap. My experience with men has me on edge nearly all the time, well, except with Beau. He calms my anxiety that I'm always fighting with inside.

"You belong to moy sin. I will do anything to keep you safe for him."

"Spaseeba." It leaves me quietly, my eyes falling to my hands.

I'm feeling unbelievably childish for making him chase down and rescue me after being somewhat ungrateful for all they've done. I should never have tried to leave. I may be a free bird, but my wings are more or less clipped. They always will be. I'm not meant to go off exploring on my own. Some may think it's weak, but it's just truth. Not all of us are meant to be strong. Some of us are weaker and the stronger ones — like Beau — balance us out.

"Nyet."

266

"No?"

"He will hear of this. Do not thank me." There's no negotiation. It's a promise, and I know Beau won't be pleased to hear about this little venture.

"Now Spartak!" I order as I hear the first explosion go off, so he'll grab Don Franchetti and stop him from escaping.

One shot to Yema's forehead and my clips empty. I don't reload, holstering and grabbing my other gun from the opposite side. It's loaded as are the other two I'm packing. With Cappeloni's death, my heart speeds up, excited one piece of scum is out of the way forever. Not very cop-like of me, but I'm no longer that person.

I won't go around killing innocent people in the future or anything, but I can easily admit that the death of these men will not weigh on my conscience. Good fucking riddance is my thinking after witnessing all the women we have the past few days. These guys are lucky Vik isn't capturing them all to torture them with his blow torch like he enjoys doing to the worst of men.

A bullet flies beside me, and I flip around quickly, finding Viktor had shot a guy behind me. This place is a goddamn madhouse with shots being fired from all directions.

"Fuck!" I shout and glare at Franchetti. His stupid men charge after us like a bunch of goddamn cowboys or something, and we have to kill them all so they don't kill us.

This is not what I wanted—at all. I was planning less casualties overall with more witnesses and freed women. I don't give a shit if the President has spoken to Tate about it or not and given his blessing with our plans. We're the lesser evil, yes, but I hate having so many dead bodies popping up everywhere. My soul is already black enough from killing the criminals I did while I was undercover. I need to concentrate on the worst of the worst.

These Italians are acting like they're at a freaking shootout in the Wild West rather than a takeover from another Boss. Hell, it's more of a takeover from all the Russians, not just one boss.

"We have to get out!" Tate yells. "Now! Reinforcements will arrive any minute, here's our window."

"The women!" I shout back as we trade fire with a few more guards. They hit the ground with all of us on them, shooting to kill. We have many more hours of training and are extra lethal when we're together like this.

"Alexei, Spartak, and Finn can help get them to the vans and the airport. Tate's right, we need to leave. We have to get to the jet with Don Franchetti while the path is clear. We may not have a better chance." Viktor agrees, and I pull the zip ties from my pocket.

Franchetti's men would check our guards at each new place, but I never let them touch my cousins or me. So we carried the equipment we needed to pull this off. Tate with the sonar devices, me with the zip ties and smoke bombs, and Viktor arranged all the backup, transportation and infiltration of our own weapons to be ready for our men to do a hostile takeover.

Shit's been crazy.

I rush toward the Don. Yanking him around, I secure his hands behind him, in the same fashion I did on the force. Once we're all boarded safely on the jet, I'll be securing his feet as well. No way am I letting this asshole get away from me now.

Jerking him along, we head out the back where we have a hummer on standby. It's reinforced to take the brunt if we come under more fire, which we do immediately as we head toward the entry gate. Viktor figured we'd need a bigger vehicle in case we ended up having to squish a bunch of us in here to escape an ambush.

One of the fuckers armed at the gate has what appears to be a mini rocket launcher propped on his shoulder, pointed at us. Franchetti laughs jovially as he sees it—stupid fucker. They won't shoot, though. We have the head of their organization with us. In Miami coming out of this mini-compound, I feel as if we should be in Cuba or something right now. These fuckers are crazier than Russian soldiers who've been up all night drinking.

"Sei uno stupido, desperato e illuso," Franchetti mutters, shaking his head.

"Did you just call me stupid?" I glare at him, and Viktor chuckles.

"He called you a fool, a desperate one," Viktor informs me, and I glare over at Franchetti again. Of course, my cousin knows multiple languages. I don't know why it never occurred to me to ask him if he knew what the hell they were saying around us.

Viktor speeds as much as he can without calling too much attention to us in the massive beast of a vehicle. We don't want the cops on us. Who knows who's in Franchetti's pocket down here. This isn't our territory.

I mean theirs; this isn't my cousin's territory. I'm becoming too comfortable, obviously.

"You'll be desperate once we're ready to extract intelligence," I mutter, peeved this cocky fucker's so smug still.

"You will get nothing," he bites out, and I slam my elbow into the side of his head, making him swear loudly.

"Oh, but we've nearly taken everything already," Tate counteracts. "We have your locations that are all being taken over as we speak, you're losing a ton of men, you haven't

270

received a penny from us nor will you. Oh yeah, and we have you and all the women. It sounds like you're a poor sport a— what do you types call it? A schmuck? Such funny names. In Russia, you'd just be called trash." He shrugs like it's the craziest thing to him and makes me chuckle.

"We'll take good care of Victoria Franchetti too. She damn sure won't be my cousin's wife either. Is she your daughter or your niece? I haven't quite figured it out yet. Regardless, we'll have fun with her." He presses on. Tate himself is an arrogant man at times.

The Don keeps his gaze trained forward and remains silent, ignoring us. He's going to be a fun one to break.

I prefer him not speaking right now. My mind's going a million miles a minute. I have a missed call from my father, and that weighs on me. He only calls if it's important when he knows I'm busy like this.

I'm sure it has to do with Sasha, and that makes me nervous, knowing she was on her own for the first time. Well, she thought she was on her own anyhow. I know my father, and he would've made sure she was overly-protected since I asked him to keep a watch on her. The thoughts still have my fingers twitching with the need to dial both of their numbers though.

With all the drama and the need to be in a hurry, it makes the trip to the private airstrip seem as if it takes forever. What is it with shit taking longer when you're in a hurry?

271

"Serpente di Masterson," Franchetti mutters, practically spitting the words as he glances in my direction for a brief second.

I have a good idea of what he said; pretty sure he just called us snakes or something. I couldn't give a fuck. I am a snake when it comes to his type of business. I hope they all suffer and I'm pleased I'll be helping bring him to our personal type of justice.

"Zatknis'," Viktor growls from the front, telling the Don to shut up in Russian. I guess he figures if the Don's going to speak in Italian, he may as well speak Russian. At least that language I actually understand.

"We're here," he says after a minute, and I release the breath I didn't realize I'd been holding these last few moments.

"The men are on their way, they just texted," Tate replies and my chest feels even less tight with the double dose of good news. I never would've been able to make it up to Finn's mother had something happened to him during all of this.

Now we just have to get Franchetti out of here and let the men take care of the captive women. The only one we weren't able to get our hands on was the Don Franchetti's brother. We'll get to him eventually; he can only hide away for so long.

We picked up Victoria Franchetti back in Russia as well. She's on a flight to us right this moment. We won't harm her, but she'll be placed under supervision at Viktor's cabin. Maybe her dear old uncle or father—whichever he is—will come out of hiding once he hears she's with us and we can nab him next. The less of the Franchetti mob out in the world, the better it'll be for everyone.

Sapphire Knight

Hearts reunited.

Sasha

I didn't think I'd missed him that badly in the week we were a part. When he comes racing into my room, my heart pounds so hard it may burst free. He looks tired, worried, and most of all beautiful — like my own exhausted dark angel.

Those words are reserved more for women I think, but it's what comes to mind when I look at him. That and warmth. This man makes me feel warm all over. My soul knows his like it's an old friend from another life.

"Beau." The word leaves me on a woosh, and then I'm in his sturdy arms, my body pressed to his. He holds me as if he can't get close enough, like I mean everything to him, as he does to me.

I'm such a fool for trying to leave, for thinking I wouldn't miss him if I left. I thought of him constantly, and I'm lucky to have his attention. After all, he could've chosen any woman at the auctions, but he picked me over them all. After the recent drama, it put things in better perspective for me. I don't ever want to lose him.

"Thank God, you're okay. Victor told me what happened while I was away. I'm so damn sorry I wasn't here to protect you."

"I'm fine. Your father stopped the men before they got to me."

"I don't know what I would've done if they took you or you were harmed." His caring words have my skin tingling all over in a pleasant way. I don't think he's mad after all. When Victor said he'd tell Beau what happened, I wasn't expecting Beau to be this way, more annoyed or fed up perhaps.

"How was your trip?"

"You're changing the subject." His face grows stern, but there's still a happy glint in his gaze.

"I don't want you to think such things, I'd rather hear about you traveling. Was Russia as beautiful as I imagine?" It feels funny asking and admitting that I can only get glimpses of my homeland.

"You don't remember it?"

"Only pieces, not much."

276

"Russia was a different experience this trip, but I promise we'll go someday and we'll see all the beautiful parts of it. We'll explore it together."

A smile breaks loose; I can't help but be excited at his promise. "And the women? Are they free?"

"Not exactly." He sighs, and my stomach flips.

"What is it?"

"We got them out of each place; there were multiple locations. But we're going to have doctors look them over before anything happens or they go anywhere. We can't just send them out in the world without making sure they have a plan or help. My cousin Tate has a large facility set up for women that go through traumatic events. It helps them readjust to regular life, and he usually finds them work so they have a way to make money legally. They are free from the horror, but they all have a long road ahead of them, that's for sure."

"Good, I'm glad your family is helping them."

"You haven't asked about *him*." It comes out with a scowl. He hates thinking about the Master. He did accuse me of loving the man after all.

"Mr. Capelloni?"

"No," he growls, not happy thinking of Yema either. "Although I did shoot him, you should know."

"Oh." I don't dare say his name. The last time was the huge fight, and I don't want to argue or cry with him right now. Hearing Yema's dead makes me want to jump around for joy. He was an evil man who hurt many people.

"Don Franchetti," he finally says.

"That's his name?"

"Yes. Do you want to know what's happened to him? What I did to him?"

"As long as you are here with me and okay, then no, I don't want to know. He is nothing to me in this life with you."

He kisses me then, his lips on mine, moving deliciously. I melt into his hard frame, giving myself over to his tenderness. His tongue swirls with mine as he embraces me to him, not letting me escape, not that I would want to leave his arms — ever.

Sweet moments pass, and he pulls away, holding my biceps, his nose lightly pressed to mine, his forehead resting on mine. He whispers, "Good because I killed him and there's no going back. You're completely mine, Sasha. None of those people exist anymore, my cousins and I took care of them."

After so many years and there's not an ounce of sadness at his proclamation toward the man known to me as Master. If anything, it's more like an imaginary weight has been lifted off my shoulders that I wasn't even aware was resting there.

And the best part of all, he called me his. Others have said it, but the seriousness in Beau's tone — in his powerful gaze — has me believing him with everything inside me. I love thinking of myself as his and him as mine too. We belong to each other.

My soul has already fused to his, and I've vowed to kill anyone who comes between us. I may be weaker than some and not a violent person, but I would change that when it comes to him. Beau is everything.

Time has passed like nothing. Six weeks gone and my body swears it needs this man to keep breathing, to keep existing, to live for once. He makes me feel free inside, and with him, it's enough.

"I'm yours," I agree, nodding as I push my lips to his chin, each cheek and then following the skin along his neck that's slightly scruffy from his lack of shaving. He's sexy like this: disheveled and needy.

His body's wound tight, no doubt ready for a release. I know how to please him, and with that, I drop to my knees in front of him. He groans, his eyes closing briefly, knowing what's about to happen—that his cock will be deep in my throat in mere moments.

I'm going to welcome him back in the best of ways I think as I undo the five buttons holding his jeans together. They're the faded Calvin Klein brand that makes his long, strong legs look as if they belong to a model.

"You're going to make me explode with that tongue; it's sinful," he mumbles, gazing down at me with heat dancing in his sparkly, hazel-colored eyes.

"You wish for me to stop?" My hands fall to my sides, and his mouth kicks up in a playful grin with my teasing.

"You stop, and I'll have to taste you first. You decide." A delicious sounding threat that I'd definitely enjoy happening.

I love his lips and tongue on me everywhere, but I want to give him pleasure first, so I pull his pants down his thighs slowly, until he steps free of them. His body is mesmerizing with the colorful swirls of ink covering him like a canvas. I've never seen so many tattoos on a person like this, and it makes him even more beautiful. I have none, so the contrast in our skin is hypnotizing.

"I think I would like to get something on me someday." I stroke his length with one hand and gesture to his ink with the other.

"Your skin is perfect, baby." He gasps with the long pull from my hands.

The bruises I had all over when I first arrived have finally gone away. A few I thought would never disappear. That's the kind of colorful patches I don't want on me. Thankfully my skin doesn't reflect them any longer, and I think a colorful tattoo of some sort would make me happy to look at each day. Maybe a dove as he calls me?

Minutes pass with me taking him far in my mouth, bringing him closer and closer to his release before he pulls me away. His tender palms push me to my back on the fluffy carpet. He switches places and practically rips my clothes off, diving between my legs. Beau's mouth on me, making me scream out a few beats later.

He's a man possessed as his tongue caresses my most sensitive parts, over and over. Beau's the best kind of lover, so giving and he reads my body like an open book. My fingers find his hair, tugging and pushing, chasing bliss with the twist of his tongue.

Tumbling through space, falling from a cliff into an ocean of waves—he makes me feel everything, eventually climbing over my frame to plunge inside my center. My pussy's raw and sated by the time he finishes loving me fully and comes up for air.

It wouldn't surprise me if the entire house got an earful from our lovemaking. I want to shout it from the rooftop that I'm his, how he cares for me enough to keep me, and that he's my *one*.

"What is it about you, my little dove? Why can't I get you out of my head? I feel you here." He places his closed fist over his heart, staring at me with a brimming intensity. I swear he can see straight through me, right into my mind and heart. He knows I'm crazy over him.

"I don't know, Beau, but I feel you there too," I reply, pulling his hand to lay over my own heart and he places a chaste kiss on my forehead before climbing to his feet. He holds his hand out to me to help me up as well. He's always taking care of me in one way or another.

"What if we both stay here or else maybe go to my cousin's house? He has a place next to a lake. I think you'd like it there too."

"Do you enjoy it there?" I ask, curious why he would take me.

"I love it. I've spoken to him about staying there more permanently. You'll have his wife and Nikoli's wife around as well. You won't feel so lonely if I have to leave and I know you'll be protected."

"If you will be happy there, then I will be too. It's not about the place, as long as you're near."

He smiles and kisses me again. He was much more reserved when he purchased me; to see him like this has me bursting with happiness and love.

"Willow, the first girl I left with, is there as well. You'll have people around that care about you, and you'll have me if you'd like, that is." It's been a long time since I've had people that care about me, besides Beau.

"What about your father?"

"We can come back to visit him if you'd like? I still haven't found Niko's sister, so I will be searching until we figure something out. My father is helping with that job as well."

"Okay. I don't want to leave him alone, much?" It's a cross between a statement and a question. I don't like asking

Beau for anything—he does so much already—but this is important. I need him to agree with me.

"We won't. But why do you feel that way?"

"He protected me when you were gone. I think he's lonely, and I don't want him to be after being kind to me."

"We'll visit, and we'll also move my mother closer."

"I can meet her?"

"Yes, I would like nothing more. She will love you."

"I hope so."

"She will."

He's giving himself to me, plus a family? After all this time, how on earth did I get so lucky?

"Let's do it." I nod excitedly.

"You've made me so happy, baby."

"You too, Beau...I've never been more happy in my life."

And it's true. He's saved me from hell and in return shown me love and light. Not only is he my man, but he's also my hero.

EPILOGUE

Krasivaya. It means beautiful,

but with strength. Unique.

-Ruta Sepetys

Two Months Later

"We'll keep looking for Natasha, Nikoli, I promise." I feel like such a fucking failure for not bringing his sister home to him. It's been so long; I honestly think she's dead. Only, I can't admit that to him. He feels guilty enough only saving one sister, hearing another may be dead could be his undoing. I hate not giving him any closure about it though.

"I know this. You are good at your job, copper."

Even months of joining with my cousins and half of them still refer to me as a cop. I don't mind though; it's a compliment. I have the utmost respect for law enforcement.

He shakes my hand and heads back toward his house he shares with Sabrina, their two children, and his sister.

We all have our own space around here, being Viktor owns so much land. It's peaceful and comforting knowing we have friends and family so close. I'm glad Sasha and I could get settled finally. We helped my mother get moved not far from here first, and everyone around here was able to meet Sasha finally.

She doesn't really understand the other women yet. It freaks her out to see them stand up to everyone so much. Sasha grew up in an entirely different kind of life, and it's taking her time to adjust to how things are now. I'm doing my best to help her process everything and not be scared of any of the other men.

My mother is trying to help too. She says Sasha reminds her of how women were back in the old Mafiya in Russia. She's soft-spoken most times and avoids confrontation. She's insanely loyal, which is one of the most important assets being affiliated with the Mafiya and Bratva. Most of all, I'm crazy in love with her, and she returns my love tenfold.

"Everything okay?" Sasha asks, coming up to where I'm still standing on the shore of the lake.

Wrapping my arms around her, I kiss her forehead. "Hi, baby. I had to tell him I haven't found his family yet."

"I'm sorry. You will find them."

"I sure hope so. It's driving me crazy."

"You are a good man, Beau."

"Spaseeba, my love," I respond, burying my nose in her shiny hair. She smells divine.

She pulls me tighter, and I mumble against her neck, "I'm going to marry you one day, Sasha."

"You are?"

"I am. I don't want to live this life without you."

"Then don't, Beau. I don't want to live mine without you either. My whole heart loves you."

She always tells me that instead of just saying the typical, 'I love you.' She makes it extra special like the regular words somehow don't mean enough for her. I think it makes me love her even more.

"I got something for you."

"You did? When?"

"Yesterday when I went with my cousins."

"What is it?" She turns to face me, her eyes lit up, excited. I've discovered my sweet woman likes presents after all and each time I surprise her, she acts like it's Christmas morning. The look is the best feeling in the world to me, besides having her affection. Best of all, too, is she's genuinely grateful. I could pick her a flower, and she treats it as if it's the most meaningful thing she's received. She says it's because it comes from me. That if it's important enough for me to give it to her, then she will treat it as gold, even if it's sand. She's fucking perfect.

I take a step back, my grin is contagious, excited to show her finally. It was so hard keeping it a secret last night, but I managed. Pushing my jeans down, I expose my hip.

"It's me?" Her eyes grow wide as she takes in the Russian style tattoo of a love bird. My cousins and Niko filled me in that it's a family thing to get a tattoo representing your other half. I happened to have my hips free from tattoos, so I decided since she's my little dove, I'd get a bird inked there in her honor. I made sure the artist used the brightest colors he had since she loves my colorful tattoos the most. It's light and beautiful, just like she is.

"The wings...Beau, they are so stunning!"

"Like you, my little dove."

"You fill my heart so full." Her eyes crest with tears, and I tug her to me, embracing her completely in my arms.

"It's because I love you with every beat of mine, Sasha, and I will forever."

And I will because she's my *one*.

Sapphire Knight

Bonus EPILOGUE

Keep some room in your heart

for the imaginable.

-Mary Oliver

Sasha

Two Years Later

"She is ours."

"Yep, all the paperwork's finally official. No one can take her from us; she's our daughter. The name change has been submitted and everything."

"Her poor mother. I thought all of the women Yema and the Don had captured were clean."

"None of us knew she had HIV until it was too late. At least her daughter—our daughter—will be taken care of. It was one less thing she had to worry about while passing."

"It's just sad that our happiness came from someone dying."

"No, our happiness comes from each other, from this little girl. Her passing was nothing we could control."

"You are right, my heart. I can't believe she will have our name. She is perfect, like her new papa."

"She is. I'm so in love with you both, Sasha," Beau whispers, getting choked up a bit as he leans his forehead against mine, gazing down at the baby hugged between us. She's 15 months old now, and we've cared for her since she took her very first breath.

I'd once believed that the Master had taken everything from me. He had my mother murdered and made my life miserable growing up. He took my choices and happiness away for so many years. He even stole from me my chance to have my own children.

When Beau and I found out I wasn't able to have babies and it was due to past trauma, I felt a little less whole. I had finally begun to heal after all the pain, and then we heard from my doctor when we decided we wanted to have a baby. I know it hurt Beau inside too, even though he was strong for me and pretended it wasn't a big deal. It was. Family is everything to him—to us—and we couldn't have our own little family. The Master had once again taken a piece of my soul away from me, and he was long gone—dead and unable to answer for his crimes.

Marianna's birth mother was one of the captives Beau helped rescue out of the Russian facility. No one knew she was pregnant; it had happened the day before Beau and his cousins showing up to save them all. When they brought her to America, they found out that not only was she carrying a baby but that she was HIV positive and had been exposed to the disease for a very long time.

Apparently, she'd tried to warn the men who stole her, but they didn't believe her. They thought it was just a made-up excuse. She was trying to stop the spread of the disease and ended up pregnant. Her sick body could barely handle the pregnancy.

The doctor begged her to terminate, but she swore it was the one positive thing to happen in her life as an adult and wouldn't give in. Her choice led us to helping to care for the baby once Marianna was born, and we fell completely in love with the perfect little bundle.

We'd put in to adopt her, but it took a long time since I didn't have any real documents that were easily attainable. Once they figured out who I was thanks to some expensive DNA testing and searching, we were able to file for a Visa and the full adoption of Marianna.

I thought with Beau my life was complete and then I laid my eyes on her and realized I didn't only have my *one*...I had *two*.

Thank you for reading Beau and Sasha's story! I hope you enjoyed their tale as much as I loved learning and writing about them. Beau was so mysterious in Unwanted Sacrifices; I knew I had to give you more of him! And Sasha was the perfect mix of broken and fire to make him realize his potential in his own family. Family isn't just blood; it's who you choose to love. Here's to finding our ones, twos, threes, fours...however many it takes to make your heart full.

XOXO

Sapphire Knight

Also by SAPPHIRE

Sapphire Knight

Standalones

Unexpected Forfeit

1st Time Love

Gangster

Stay up to date with Sapphire

Email

authorsapphireknight@yahoo.com

Website

www.authorsapphireknight.com

Facebook

www.facebook.com/AuthorSapphireKnight

Made in the USA
San Bernardino, CA
09 July 2018